Married To The Military

Women share the experience
of loneliness, helplessness
and desperation as their
husbands complete their
military commitment.

Married To The Military

Women share the experience of loneliness, helplessness and desperation as their husbands complete their military commitment.

From the Editors
Of *True Story* And
True Confessions

Published by True Renditions, LLC

True Renditions, LLC
105 E. 34th Street, Suite 141
New York, NY 10016

ISBN: 978-1-938877-60-5

Visit us on the web at www.truerenditionsllc.com.

Contents

ARMY WIFE'S MARRIAGE GUIDE, MILITARY-STYLE!
For all those homeland women out there who're fighting the war on terror, one pile of paperwork at a time. . . .

When I married my husband, there was no doubt that we both spoke English. Although on occasion he does lapse into Man-Speak and sometimes I need to reference the Man-Speak-To-English Dictionary to understand that "I'll be there in fifteen minutes," really means: "I'll be there in about an hour after you remind me three more times that we're running late."

I admit I'm not perfect and sometimes I forget that he doesn't understand Woman-Talk and I have to translate, "Fine," to mean: "I'm simply agreeing with you to end this discussion. I'm still right and you're being an idiot for questioning me." But it was not until he was deployed to Iraq that the language barrier between us became decidedly pronounced.

While stationed in Heidelberg, Germany, my husband's military obligations required him to go to Iraq, leaving me responsible for maintaining our household. This had been expected, of course, and we had planned for the separation. What we had not counted on was that our duty station would change during his deployment. The task of satisfying all of the military requirements of a PCS fell to me.

A PCS?

This was my first exposure to the language of my husband: Army-Speak.

A Permanent Change of Station is what I had to accomplish. It was to be an eye-opening experience. I was in the weeds without a weed whacker or an operator's manual and I didn't even know the language.

The first item on "The Checklist From Hell" is to obtain an RFO. What is that, you might ask? It is a Request for Orders. The Army does not do anything without ORDERS.

Unfortunately, I have no idea about where to go for an RFO. I contact the civilian worker in my husband's office and she tells me she'll send me an OP MOVE order. This is different from a regular PCS and the best I can figure is that an OP MOVE happens when you're moving within a foreign country. The OP MOVE order begins the process of clearing the duty station. Unfortunately, the Housing

Department (we were living in military quarters at the time) is not satisfied with OP MOVE orders because they're not official ORDERS, nor do they reflect the detachment date from CONUS. CONUS? What is that? Turns out CONUS is Army-Speak for Continental United States, of course.

During my quest for ORDERS, the Army inevitably slips a twist into my mission. It is decided, sometime after I obtain the RFO, that my husband will not be going to the planned unit of 1-77 AR BN, but now will be going to 1-4 CAV. What is the difference? I have no idea. All I know is that suddenly, I have to start over at step one with a new RFO.

The new RFO arrives, except that it is not the RFO. I receive my husband's ORB, instead. It is interesting to read, the Officer Record Brief, as it delineates his military history, but still—it is not the all-important RFO. Back to step one.

Eventually the amended OP MOVE RFO arrives and I am instructed to go to the PSB. With it in hand, I venture to the PSB. At the time, of course, I have no idea what that is, but that is where I am going, nonetheless. Well, it turns out that the PSB is the Personnel Support Battalion and they inform me that I need to have a DA Form 31 (Department of Army Form 31) before I can request ORDERS. So, back to the unit for a DA Form 31 (Request and Authority for Leave), where I am told that it must be signed by the G3 and my husband. Of course, both of them are in Baghdad, which is why I'm doing all of this in the first place.

Needless to say, this is the point where I commence with begging. Tears of frustration translate into Man-Speak as: "Oh, please help me! I am in distress and I need a big, strong man to rescue me!"

And it works! The acting G3 (I am still not sure what that means or who that is) signs the DA Form 31 and he even allows me to sign for my husband and attach a copy of the POA (Power of Attorney). Making progress. Now I have the amended RFO and a signed DA Form 31. I should be good, right?

Nope.

Not good.

The PSB people tell me that I have to go to the STB PAC office to get a control number and a commander's signature. As I am without an Army/English Dictionary, I struggle with the language barrier. Eventually, I discover that STB is the Special Troops Battalion, but PAC is still a mystery to me to this day.

I get to the STB PAC with all my papers in hand. I have done everything I have been instructed to do. Now, may I have the ORDERS, please?

Nope.

This is when I learn that the STB PAC office submits the DA Form 31 and copy of RFO to the PSB to get ORDERS. The process will take approximately two weeks. So, I return home, confused and feeling like a stranger in a strange land.

Shortly after I arrive at the familiarity of my home, the telephone rings. I am given instructions to bring the POA and copy of the signed DA Form 31 to the LEVY BRIEFING and, most importantly—Do NOT be late.

Sure. No problem.

What is a LEVY BRIEFING?

Thankfully, fate intervenes and my husband calls me from Iraq to check on the status of the ORDERS. I describe to him how I've been trying to clear the thick underbrush and resistant dandelions with the gardening equivalent of fingernail clippers.

"Oh, and by the way," I ask, "what's a LEVY BRIEFING?"

LEVY BRIEFING translates Army to Man-Speak as: "To sit in a mandatory meeting for about an hour and listen to instructions on the necessary steps that must be taken in order to facilitate a change of station." That translates from Man-Speak to Woman-Talk as: "To go to some dumb meeting that your husband should be going to and listen to some soldier drone on and on about all the steps you've already taken so that you can get the ORDERS." Yeah—

The ORDERS I still don't have!

After several days of running around and frantic phone calls to my mother, a long-time, long-suffering Army wife, asking rhetorical questions like, "Why does the Army do it this way?" and "Why does it have to be so complicated?", the elusive ORDERS arrive . . . along with my husband! Boy, am I glad to see him. Now he can take on the PCS task. Phew!

Needless to say, the experience was an education. I added a few acronyms to my vocabulary—to say the least. Additionally, I learned that when my husband says, "I love you," he really means: "Thank you for being with me and putting up with everything. You're the greatest and I love you more than you can imagine. Thanks for going Army."

When I say, "I love you," to my husband, I mean: "Baby, I love you with all of my heart and soul. I'm even willing to learn a whole, new language just so that I can understand you better and love you even more."

THE END

My husband is in Iraq
AND I'M PREGNANT AND
AFRAID TO TELL HIM

I can't handle this!

I was standing at the large window, but not actually noticing anything outside. I'd spent much of the past two days and nights here in the hospital's pediatric intensive care unit—and the reports were still not good.

Judith, our bright, loving, delightful little two-year-old was lying here, still unconscious, still on the "extremely serious" list—and her six-year-old sister, Melanie, was with our next-door neighbors, Neda and Patrick Black.

I should be home with Melanie! I thought. They insist she's doing okay, but I know how sensitive she is. When I was with her for a while last evening, she clung to me—begging me not to leave again. I read several of her favorite children's stories to her and stayed until she went to sleep—but I didn't know how she'd be when she woke up and found I wasn't there. Again.

I'd call later to see if she slept through the night—which she'd been unable to do after seeing her little sister hit by that car, right out in front of our house. . . .

I turned as Pastor Cleve Hollister, one of the chaplains at this large community hospital, came into the room—his ever-ready smile lighting his face.

I responded to his cheerful, "Good morning!" as I started toward him, but he picked up the straight chair beside Melanie's crib and carried it to place near the recliner in which I'd spent the night. "Were you able to sleep, Marnie?"

"Not much. . . ."

"Better than the night before?"

"Well, perhaps some. . . ."

"Good! And the nurses seem encouraged by Judith's condition."

His words gave some encouragement, yet I sighed.

"I feel so—alone going through this without Randy."

He leaned over and put his hand on my arm. "Does your husband know what you're going through?"

I shook my head. "I'd have liked to notify him right away—but he already feels so bad about not being with us—having to be in Iraq instead of here with his family! . . ."

"That's what I understood." As I sat down in the recliner, he seated himself on the chair he'd just moved.

4

"I'd—so hoped he wouldn't have to go—but he did join ROTC and got financial help with going through college, so we knew there was a probability of his being called."

"How long has he been gone?"

"That happened more than three and a half months ago—and I've been praying and praying. . . ."

He listened patiently, nodding, and occasionally putting in some comment or question. And then, I shared something I hadn't yet told even my parents or friends. "I've got another problem, too—you see, I—I'm pregnant and. . . ."

His slight smile seemed tentative—which I suppose was natural, since he'd wonder why that should be a problem. "What has your husband said about this?"

Tears formed, and I impatiently brushed them away. "I—haven't told him yet."

As he was obviously waiting for me to continue, I explained about my miscarriage less than a year ago. ". . . And I'm so scared I'm about to have another one; I've been cramping and spotting for over a week."

"What does your doctor say about that?"

That was similar to what he'd asked concerning Randy. "I haven't got to see him. When I called right at the beginning, Dr. Danforth was at some medical conference or something—there was just a recorded message about the office being closed. Then, with Judith's accident, well . . . by the time I did get through, yesterday, there was no available appointment time until Thursday."

"You left a message when you first tried to call, didn't you?"

"I—should have, but didn't," I admitted, then added, "There didn't seem quite as much cramping last night—but it's back again this morning. . . ."

"What about the bleeding?"

"That's continuing."

"Today?"

"Um-hmmm. . . ."

He leaned forward in his chair, as though to say something else, but I added, "Doctor Danforth delivered both of our girls, and we like him—and he helped Randy and me a whole lot when I had that miscarriage."

I sighed. "I hadn't meant to get pregnant again so soon."

I'd paused, and he asked gently, "Had he suggested taking precautions for a time?"

"Well, yes, and we did—but then, with Randy's imminently being shipped out."

It wasn't more than fifteen minutes after the chaplain left when

5

Dr. Danforth came into the room, asking, "How's your little one, Marnie?"

"The pediatrician says she's doing 'as well as can be expected,' but I haven't seen much change."

"Well, I just talked with Chaplain Jim, and that's what he gathered, too." He shifted position before asking, "What about you, my girl? I understand you're having the same symptoms as before?"

I sat up straighter—afraid he might be provoked at my not having left a message. However, he remained calm and friendly, in addition to being professionally serious as I shared symptoms and concerns.

He'd been the physician to order my pregnancy test four weeks after Randy had to go, and he called the results—and he was now asking questions. Before he left, he said I should come to the office that morning; even though I didn't have an appointment, he wanted to check me immediately, and perhaps start some medication.

I did as he requested, then I stopped at the pharmacy before going back across town to pick up Melanie. By that time, I'd decided it was best to tell the neighbors about my own situation, and Neda assured me that if I needed to go to the hospital in the middle of the night—like last time, or could use help with caring for Melanie, or anything—I was to call them, whether it was day or night.

She insisted that I eat lunch with them. Back in my own kitchen, I phoned our pastor, Rev. Lee Garland, and asked that an update of our situation be put on the church's prayer chain—that Judy continued to need prayers. Though supposedly she was "doing as well as could be expected," she'd still not regained consciousness.

And I, also, needed prayers for my physical problems.

It was comforting to know that within an hour, people in thirty-four different households would be praying for us!

Pastor Lee and Penny, his wife, came to our house as soon as they'd passed on my request. They had encouraged—well, insisted—that I put through a call to my husband as quickly as possible. After all, with so many others learning of my physical difficulty, it was all too probable that Randy would hear of it from others—and he'd have every right to be upset. So my not wanting to worry him would be fruitless my ". . . not wanting to worry him."

I had difficulty figuring out what time it was in Iraq, but when I couldn't reach Randy at either of the numbers I had, I asked the operator if I could be connected with the chaplain of his division. That took a while, but when I finally spoke to someone in his unit, he got Colonel Mitchell to the phone.

The officer seemed approachable enough for me to explain my situation, and why I needed to speak with my husband. He even left his personal connection open while trying to expedite it.

6

When that wasn't accomplished, however, I found myself on the verge of tears. He then asked if it was okay for him to relay my message and say I'd like him to call home as soon as possible. I told him I'd appreciate that. I also gave him the number of the room in which Judy presently was—and also of the hospital switchboard—just in case she'd be moved out of intensive care.

When asked for information about getting in touch with my obstetrician, I momentarily fretted that he didn't believe me—that he might've suspected that I was lying or trying to "pull something." But then, realizing he was only doing his job, I gave him that phone number and address in addition to my own and our pastor—and I tried to reassure myself as I hung up that he thought Randy would want to talk with one or both of them.

Neda insisted that I eat with her, Melanie, and their daughter, Marianne. I did so—then I felt awful when my daughter cried as I left to go back to the hospital.

I hadn't thought too much about the bleeding and cramping until I got back in the car. Not remembering what music I'd played the last time, I just pushed in the disk—which turned out to be exactly what I needed: "Let Not Your Heart Be Troubled," sung by a group at our church the very last Sunday before my husband left.

The message of those words came through to me even more poignantly than when I'd originally heard them. I hummed along and paid special attention—not just to the skill of the musicians, but to the words.

Judy was lying on her side in her crib when I arrived, her back to the doorway. I wonder if they just turned her, I thought. I remembered that I'd rolled her onto her other side before leaving. As I stood there for a moment before entering the room, I saw her little hand move several inches across the sheet—and rest on "Cuddle-baby," her very favorite, though worse-for-wear-and-countless-trips-through-the-washing-machine cloth doll my mother made and sent to her for her very first birthday.

Oh, thank-You, God! I prayed silently as I walked around the foot of the crib. Her eyes were open. As she heard or sensed my presence, she rolled over onto her back and looked right at me.

And smiled! "Hi, Mommy. . . ."

I was ecstatic, but I forced myself to act as naturally as possible.

"Hi, Judy," I responded as I went up along the other side. "How's my sweetie?"

She started to push herself up to a sitting position, but then, seeming surprised or puzzled, she started picking at the cast on her left arm.

"It's stuck, Mommy."

I quickly crossed to push the call-button left for me to ring during the night should a nurse be needed, but I kept talking to Judy. As I lowered the side of the crib, Maryse Langley, one of our church members—a nurse in that ward—responded.

I was blessedly surprised at Judy's rousing so completely, as though just waking from an afternoon nap or a normal night's sleep. We were all talking at once, especially Judy, not wanting that pesky thing "stuck on my arm."

She didn't seem upset about being in a strange place and, since she'd known Maryse all her life, even the things being done, getting her to respond verbally and physically, seemed like fun games to her.

Maryse left for a few minutes, and I later learned—as I'd suspected—that she'd gotten the good news out to the pediatrician, as well as to the other nurses of this unit. When she returned, she asked if Judy would like something to drink. When the apple juice went down with no difficulty, the intravenous feeding tubes were also removed.

Judy wasn't too happy with that procedure, and I probably wouldn't have been either, because it did hurt a little. Soon, she was eating a few bites of watermelon after my mentioning that to be her very favorite food.

We didn't let her see herself in a mirror right away. Though I was very aware of her long hair having been shaved off prior to surgery, she didn't immediately discover that—nor even complain of that area being sore.

I waited until I went back home to tell Neda the good news while picking up Melanie. Later, while soup was warming for supper, I called our pastor, requesting that he put a follow-up message on the prayer chain, giving the good news about Judy. I also added my sincere thanks for the prayers, and my praise to God.

Things were so much better that, though I did have to change my pad, I wasn't even thinking much about the off-and-on cramping. I'd just finished reading a story to Melanie when the phone rang.

"Hi, sweetheart," that familiar, loving voice greeted. "How are things going, today? Any better?"

"Oh, Randy!" Even though I'd been praying for this call, I could hardly believe it was possible! "Judy just woke up this morning, and seems—well, much like always. And Melanie and I just ate together here at the house and read a book and—and. . . ."

I stopped, wondering, "Are things okay with you?"

"They are, now. I was pretty shook up, though, when the chaplain just told me how rough things have been for you. I was out on duty for the past thirty-six hours, so I just got word of your trying to reach me."

"Was it a—bad thirty-six hours?" I asked, though knowing

he wouldn't be allowed to talk about many things he was doing or experiencing.

"Pretty rough, actually—but hearing your voice and getting this good news makes all the difference in the world!"

We talked for another minute or two before he asked, "Any change as to your physical problems, dear?"

I hated to worry him, but he did need to know. "Not really. The pains aren't unbearable, but the cramps and the bleeding are so very much like those last days before the miscarriage that—well— I'll confess that it's worrisome."

He sighed. "The chaplain and a couple others here have already talked with our minister and your doctor and Judith's pediatrician. It seems like they're trying to see if it's possible for me to come home for a week or so."

"Oh, Randy! Oh, darling, that would be so wonderful!"

There was the slightest of pauses before he said, somewhat hesitantly, "Perhaps I shouldn't have said anything yet about this, but—I just had to talk with you and let you know that we're trying our very best to work things out. . . ."

We talked for another couple minutes before he said, "Look, dear, I'm going to have to hang up because there are several other guys waiting for this phone. I will call you tomorrow—or the next day at the very latest.

"You take care of yourself—for all our sakes."

"I will; I promise," I assured him. "And you do likewise! . . ."

"I love you more than you can possibly imagine!"

Tears were rolling down my cheeks, but I tried not to let him know that, "Oh, yes, dear, I do know how much—as much as I love you!"

He did not, however, call the next day or the following one. When he finally did call three days later, he could only say: "There was no way I could get in touch. Things were much too hectic. But I'm back now."

Back now. He must have been doing something he wasn't allowed to share with me—and I'd been married to him long enough to know it was something big. "You are . . . okay?"

"Yes, Marnie, I'm okay—especially so when talking with the woman I love."

He asked then how I was doing, and I had to say that things were no better, "But they're not much worse, either," I added.

"In what way are they worse?"

"Well," I almost wished I hadn't worded my response like that, "the cramps seem to be stronger, and sometimes, they're—well, somewhat regular."

9

"You've talked with the doctor, haven't you?"

"Yes, of course. And he's told me to be careful, not to do any lifting or heavy work—even, when possible, not to carry the girls or heavy grocery bags.

"I'm not sure how much good it will do, but I'm sure trying to be good . . . ."

It was only two days later when he called again—this time much more cheerful and excited.

"Guess what, Marnie! I'm flying home in one of the military planes—I can't tell you any more than that over the phone, but I will call when I arrive in the States."

Needless to say, I hardly left the house for the next three days—and I was almost bowled over when he arrived in a rental car. Melanie was the one who saw the vehicle coming into our driveway and, shouted, "Daddy's home!" dashing out the front door.

He gathered her into his arms and strode across the lawn to where I was coming toward them, holding onto Jen's hand to keep her from running and possibly falling.

He could only stay a week, but what a blessing his presence was! His major concern was that I get a lot of rest, so he took the girls with him everywhere he went—the longest trips being to his parents and to mine.

He insisted that I spend most of my time in bed or sitting back in the recliner or occasionally, on a kitchen chair as he prepared meals and even did a couple loads of laundry!

Whether all that tender loving care is what made the difference, or if it was all those prayers people continued to raise—or maybe just his presence. But by the time he had to leave, I was no longer bleeding much, and the cramps were much less severe.

Yes, it was rough for all of us when he went back, but we'd truly enjoyed one another to the fullest.

Without my having any part in it, several of our good friends at church made up a list of volunteers—almost all of whom were part of the prayer chain. Each of the women, or couples, had volunteered to come to our house during the afternoons, with the express order that I spend at least a couple of hours in bed.

Those people ranged in age from Kelly Rogers, in her midteens to Granny Cogdell, who was in her early nineties. Many of them brought meals or meal-starters, like Granny's couple pounds of hamburger browned with onions, along with a very large jar of spaghetti sauce—and also a box of pasta, and can of kidney beans.

"Do whatever you'd like, dear," she told me, "but you might consider having just some of the meat-and-onions the first meal, then add the spaghetti sauce to what's left for another, and the kidney beans and chili powder to finish it off."

10

Several of the volunteers also brought their children or grandchildren with them, much to the delight of my kids. And several of the men and teens showed up either with their tractor-mowers or push ones, while others—including even Granny Cogdell and some of the younger folks—cleared weeds from the flower beds and around trees.

And now, as I'm finishing my account, I want to tell you that I've just come home from the hospital with our darling little Leland. He was born just a few days before his official due-date, weighing in at five pounds and fifteen ounces—almost as much as Judy's six pounds and three ounces weight at birth.

His sisters adore him as much as we, his parents, do—and we're eagerly awaiting his daddy's coming home permanently—which should be just seven weeks from now.

We can hardly wait to all be together, our family complete.

But something else has become very important to us. Through all these trying days, we've been reminded again and again that the term "family" need not be restricted to just those having close genetic lines.

Randy and I have lived in this town ever since we were married, almost nine years ago, and we've gone to our church and been members during all that time. We've been happy there, and have grown spiritually—but it's only now that we've become truly aware of actually being in a "church family," with some people even closer than many flesh-and-blood ones.

Yes, we have grown spiritually, but also in love for one another, and I've promised God that I will not, in the future, let myself become too filled with my own busy-ness and selfishness that I don't have time or energy to reach out to others.

THE END

BATTALION WIFE
Before I Knew It, I Was Caught Up In A
Web Of Deception And Secrets!

I put down my novel and glanced over at Brad in the seat next to me. Sound asleep! How in the world could the man snooze in the confines of an airplane seat with that cold air blowing on his face?

Brad was lost in dreamland. Dinner was being served a few rows ahead of us, and I wondered if he wanted to eat. Breakfast would be served just before we landed in Frankfurt, Germany. At least we'd lucked out with a civilian flight, so Brad could wear comfy faded jeans and a sweatshirt and not have to worry about wrinkling up his dress greens. If only the good vibes would stay with us in our new assignment.

As I sampled my baked fish in its indescribable sauce, my mind wandered back to our marriage six years earlier. It was a simple ceremony, performed by Brad's division chaplain. Only our parents were in attendance. Brad was career army all the way. He'd never made that a secret from me. Just back from a hardship tour in Korea before he met me, he was certain of all his overseas commitments were behind him, and he'd just coast along in the nation's capital until retirement. Face it: Washington, D.C. was a dream assignment.

Once he reached twenty years of active duty, he could retire. He was nearing sixteen years. In a way, I envied him—not that I'd ever consider enlisting in the army. How many career fields allowed a guy to retire at age forty? That was the best part, though I couldn't imagine Brad as retired. Retirement was for old people.

I was a corporate secretary and months away from a major promotion to office manager, when Brad announced we were headed to Germany. I recalled how my first reaction was there had to be some sort of mistake. He and I felt so settled in the nation's capital, and we'd been socking away savings to put down a deposit on a two-bedroom, brick townhouse half an hour away in Northern Virginia.

As I read his overseas assignment orders, I felt the rug was being yanked out from under me. What about my great job? What about all our friends? Our future townhouse in Alexandria? I was born and raised in Washington, D.C., and I couldn't imagine living elsewhere.

As Brad showed me the letter from his sponsor—a friendly-sounding Sergeant Lakeland, who promised he would help us settle in comfortably—Brad told me to try to remain optimistic. He admitted he was as surprised as I was about the assignment. As he put it, "Look, when duty calls, I have to put on my cap and go. No soldier can refuse Uncle Sam!"

Sergeant Lakeland had sent us an assortment of maps, brochures, and information about the area. He would be the man who picked us up at the airport when we flew in, with the keys to our living quarters in his pocket. Sergeant Lakeland would handle everything. At least, we had someone on our side. I sighed and put down my fork. I never savored eating while strapped into an airplane seat. My thoughts wandered back to when I'd met my husband at an outdoor concert seven years earlier. My parents liked him immediately, but warned me military life would be no piece of cake.

What did they know about it? Nobody in my family had ever served, and all they really understood about it was from the movies—which were mostly about World War II. Back in the old days, as Brad told me, you understood exactly who the enemy was. Today, with terrorism peering around every corner and everyone being on edge all the time, the enemy seemed almost invisible. Soldiers had even more reason to stay on their toes.

Some hours later, yawning and sleepy-eyed, Brad and I deplaned. We hoped we could hook up right away with Sergeant Lakeland and our luggage. We lost out on both counts.

As it turned out, Sergeant Lakeland had a death in his immediate family back in Texas. Since he was on emergency leave in Austin, another man in Brad's battalion came to pick us up. He was all smiles—straight out of a recruitment poster, I thought. He helped us to the missing luggage counter to file a claim when one of our bags didn't come through.

He seemed very efficient, and told us he knew exactly where our housing was. He nosed the green sedan into the parking lot, unloaded our single suitcase from the trunk, then handed a ring of keys to Brad. He told us to enjoy the German holiday weekend, and for Brad to report to work in three days time. He pointed to the left, and told Brad the battalion headquarters was located four or five minutes away—an easy stroll.

We waved good-bye as the only person we knew in the entire country drove off.

To say our temporary quarters appeared dreary would be an understatement. From the outside, the building was nothing but chips where blue paint had once been as well as terra cotta roof tiles that reminded me of a gingerbread house. A scruffy, almost leafless, hedge ran between the parking area and the front of the building. The corner garden was all but abandoned. A yellow telephone booth completed the landscape. It wasn't exactly cozy.

Brad unlocked the front door.

13

"Relax, hon; it's only for a few months," he said. "We'll be in our permanent housing way before Christmas."

Was that supposed to make me feel better? Anyway, I couldn't imagine dragging a Christmas tree up dozens of steps. We were assigned to the fourth floor—which was really nothing but a decorated attic. The ceilings sloped, and the windows were tiny. The three-bedroom unit was furnished with mismatched furniture that looked like it had been purchased at a garage sale.

All the bedrooms had twin beds! Could things get any worse?

The kitchen was barren, with a fold-up table and three rickety chairs. The stove and fridge, while clean, came from my mother's generation. I couldn't help but picture the custom, built-in kitchen in the model townhouse in Northern Virginia. I opened the cupboard over the metal sink and found a few cups and saucers and an iron skillet. There were two chipped plates on the counter. That was it? Sergeant Lakeland's letter had assured us the quarters were fully furnished, and all our basic needs would be met until our shipment of household goods showed up.

Where was the flatware? I opened three drawers. How were we supposed to eat in this place?

Brad disappeared for a few seconds and came back with airline packets.

"These came with our coffees this morning. Relax, at least we have plastic spoons."

I had to laugh. It was the military preparedness that had been drilled into him. Brad could handle anything in a pinch!

"We can eat soup!" he suggested.

"Did you bring soup from our flight, too?" I asked.

Brad shrugged.

"'Fraid not. Look, we can go out to eat. What time is it? Maybe, we can get a pizza."

I wasn't used to not having access to a car. I wasn't used to living in the attic in a foreign country, either. I stared at Brad. Did he expect us to walk in a strange town, possibly for miles, until we happened to find a pizzeria open on a holiday afternoon?

"Let's ask a neighbor," Brad suggested.

He knocked on the only other apartment on our floor, but nobody answered. He tried the bell. Still, no response.

Together, we ventured down a flight of stairs and went to every door. Either everybody was at work, or the apartments were not occupied. It was starting to feel a little spooky, us living all alone in an attic and not having so much as a telephone.

Brad found nobody at home on the second and first floors, either.

"I think we've got the whole building to ourselves," he said. "Our personal villa."

14

We could make love in the hallway! Why that bizarre idea popped into my head, I had no idea. One look at the ugly brown tile with a light layer of dust, peeling and yellowed wallpaper, and the wilting potted plants on the windowsills, it was not exactly a romantic setting. True, the hallway light was muted. The light bulbs in the hallway were low wattage. Some sort of military money-saving madness, no doubt.

"Maybe the building's condemned!" I said. Even I wasn't certain it was a joke. Maybe it was condemned.

We hiked across the street to a base, called a kaserne. Pizza was nowhere to be found, but we settled for simple cafeteria fare, and we could use dollars. We both had euros in our wallets. We'd have to get used to the blue and brown shades of the foreign currency. "Funny money" is what Sergeant Lakeland had called it in his correspondence.

After we ate, we found a convenience store and stocked up so our refrigerator would have something in it besides ice cube trays—at least, a few basics. We even found a package of inexpensive camping flatware, not perfect, but it would have to suffice.

When we carried our sacks back to our condemned housing, I was glad Brad carried a pocket flashlight. We didn't know where the switch was for the outdoor lighting. The hallway was dim, so Brad walked ahead of me and shone the flashlight side-to-side for safety. As we got to our door, Brad turned to me and asked, "Do you want me to carry you across the threshold?"

I giggled. This was the fun-loving man I knew—the one who wasn't preoccupied with the demands of army life. The Brad I married didn't eat, sleep, and drink military regulations. Sure, he was a "lifer," a career man, but he worked his hours and drove home. At least, that had been our routine in the nation's capital.

First, he carried our grocery bags to the kitchen and then he returned for me. As I wrapped my arms around my husband's wide shoulders, and we entered our new living quarters, I hoped Germany would turn out to be a second honeymoon for us.

He set me down in the living room. I located a light switch. What an ugly room! For Brad's sake, I would do my best to look on the bright side of things and not bother him with petty complaints. Brad's career required he put his life on the line, and that's what mattered most. Brad hoped he'd have an office job, same as in Washington. He'd been a squad leader, sometimes an acting platoon sergeant. He'd worked eight-to-five. That was what military life in Washington, D.C. was all about: desk work with weekends and holidays free.

Somehow, we both feared this overseas adventure could turn out to be a completely different story.

The next morning, we knew from the sounds of car engines

starting up, that the building across the road was occupied. Ours might be condemned, but that was not the fate of all the buildings on our street.

I asked Brad why those people had to work on a holiday, and he didn't. His voice thick with sleep, he said they could be medics or military police.

I looked at our travel alarm clock. It was six-twenty. Too early for me! Brad was already snoring away. Did he remember it was my twenty-ninth birthday? The mattress of the narrow bed was too soft. Back home, we'd slept in a king-sized bed—one with a firm mattress. We were told it could be up to three months before the ship brought our household belongings. I looked around the sparse bedroom, with our open suitcase perched on the dresser. The heavy green curtains were an unsuitable match for the red carpet and pumpkin orange bedspreads. Was I dreaming, or had I awakened in the wrong décor?

Hours later, when Brad woke up, I was in the kitchen scrambling us some eggs. With no coffee pot, we had to be happy with instant. I laughed as I set the chipped plates and our camping eating utensils on the table. Some birthday!

Brad buttered us some rye bread. We had no toaster. From his robe pocket, he extracted a tiny box.

Brad had remembered my birthday after all! Just the thought almost brought tears to my eyes. First, I kissed the man in my life; then, I opened the velvety box—which contained a heart-shaped locket on a long chain. It was engraved, I love you no matter where on earth we are.

My sweet Brad! Maybe this assignment would be our second honeymoon, after all. We didn't need fancy silverware or matching dishes to be happy, did we?

Once Brad became absorbed learning his new job duties and trying to remember all the names and ranks of the guys in his unit, he had less time for me. He was attending a course to learn European road signs for a driver's license, and he brought the study guides home for me to review in my spare time.

Spare time? Who was the man kidding? I'd given up the job I loved. I had no car, no television, no radio, no computer. Not even a phone. I didn't know a soul. The community pool was under construction. I hadn't found the library, yet. All the plants in the garden were long dead. My mother was three thousand miles away.

A few times, the tears came. I reminded myself I should feel proud to be a military spouse. Self-pity leads nowhere. Let the other wives in the battalion bother their husbands with complaints. I would stay strong.

Being inside our four walls alone most of the time, wasn't for me. That was clear! One day, I boldly marched across the street to the building that wasn't condemned. I knocked on doors and met most of the women of my new neighborhood—primarily moms with kiddies underfoot. Everybody asked for my telephone number, but I had to explain over and over that we had no phone. I invited everybody over for coffee the next day, and hoped I had enough cups to comply.

The first door I'd knocked at was where Sylvia lived. About my age, she came from suburban Chicago. She told me she'd been an accountant before their recent assignment to Germany. "I'm so sorry we ladies didn't come over to welcome you two," she said. "Usually, we show up with cake and a friendly handshake, but nobody realized your building was occupied. We thought it was being renovated. My husband said the other night he thought he saw a light on in there." Sylvia had her hands full, keeping up with her twins, who were making the most of the "terrible twos." She took time to wrap up a couple of thick slices of still-warm banana bread for me to take home.

The next door was answered by Anna-Maria, a German citizen. Her husband was a tanker, and their baby was a year old, with another on the way. She'd been working in one of Germany's top casinos when she met her future husband, she told me. He was on a Black Forest tour, a battalion-sponsored trip.

When I told Anna-Maria I hadn't seen much of the area yet, she answered, "Sylvia and I can give you a quickie tour of the housing area if it ever stops raining. If you're brave enough, you can practice buying a bus ticket. I can teach you some German words and phrases if you want." She gave me a nonfiction book about culture shock and living abroad. "Just return it whenever you're finished," she said, warmly. "You know where I live!"

Michelle, at thirty-six, was the oldest. She opened her door wide, gave me a tour of their quarters—even of their closets—and offered to share some of her magazines on the spot. "I'm an army widow, but in the good sense of the word," she said, laughter creeping into her voice. Her medic husband spent more days a year in the field than at home. Their three children were junior high age and Michelle toyed with the idea of getting a job at the PX. I could well understand her longing to get out of the house. Some days, I missed getting dressed up in my office attire and driving to my former job.

The following morning, my doorbell rang punctually at ten o'clock. Three women, all dressed in jeans or jogging suits, had responded to my invitation.

As we sat on my faux leather couch and I passed out coffee, I realized I'd forgotten milk and sugar. What sort of hostess was I?

I headed to the kitchen and Michelle called out after me, "Not to worry, girl. I keep my flask right here next to my heart!"

17

I thought she was joking, but when I returned, Michelle was pouring what smelled like whiskey into her coffee cup.

"Hold the sugar," she instructed.

I was getting an eyeful and an earful! The reason another neighbor hadn't shown up was her husband had left for the field, today.

I didn't get it.

"So why can't she join us for coffee if she's alone?" I asked.

Michelle laughed. "She's not alone, dearie—if you catch my drift."

She added a generous swig of the hard stuff to her coffee. Then, she laughed even louder.

Sylvia and Anna-Maria joined in her laughter. Sylvia finished off the chocolate chip cookies she'd brought. When she finished one package, she got another out of her purse and slapped it on the coffee table. She wasted no time helping herself to a handful.

As I watched Sylvia lick her fingers and listened to the chuckles all around me, I felt left out of a private joke.

Anna-Maria explained, "See, it's sort of an army tradition overseas. When hubby's away, wifey will play. Go look out your picture window. See the closed blinds over in our building? Her boyfriend's already moved in—suitcase and all! Don't let on, but none of her kids looks anything like Daddy!"

The trio laughed again. I was having a hard time following everything. I peered out the front window and asked, "Is it the third floor?"

"No," answered Sylvia. "Those are the nudists. Look at the second floor. That's the one who runs around."

I tried not to gasp. Had military life in Washington been this way? Maybe so. I wasn't sure. I hadn't witnessed it up close because we'd always rented an apartment quite a distance from where Brad worked. Most of my friends had come from my office or our apartment complex. They weren't military families. I wondered if all the battalion wives were harboring such dirty secrets, compulsions, or nasty habits. Could it be?

Anna-Maria caught the girls up on the latest shoplifters among the battalion wives, and Michelle told us who was in jail and who'd be let out.

Hours later, as Brad and I sat down to our meat loaf supper, I was enthusiastic in telling him all about Sylvia, Anna-Maria, and Michelle. Just knowing I had prospective friends across the street, made me feel a little less stranded—even if they were a trio of crazies.

Brad appeared amused by my account and said he knew all their husbands—at least, by sight. "I also know that Anna-Maria and her

18

husband are big-time gamblers: high-stakes poker, even roulette if they can find it. The word around the headquarters is they've lost some six or seven thou this year, alone!"

My eyebrows shot up at that one. That's a ton of money! I recounted to Brad how she'd asked me if we had any quarters, in the house. When I gave her change for three dollars, she'd thanked me twice. Very enthusiastically.

Brad nodded. "Slot machines. They've got them on base in all the clubs–junior enlisted, NCO, and officers. I'm pretty sure some take nickels and others quarters."

Go figure. How I wished we had our computer so I could e-mail Mom. She'd get such a kick out of hearing about our misfit neighbors.

"It's starting to sound like a pretty wild neighborhood around here," Brad said, "but realize the bad apples are not even ten percent of the military population. You just notice the troublemakers more. I'm sure the rest of the families residing here are as boring or as normal as we are!"

My Brad could always make me smile. Of course, he was right. I was jumping to conclusions. I couldn't judge the entire combat engineer battalion after meeting just a few family members.

After we ate, he handed me a bulging plastic bag. "I forgot to tell you. Our first batch of mail got forwarded from back home. I got this from the battalion mailroom, today."

That had to be a lucky signal of some sort, our first mail in more than five weeks. Eagerly, I sorted through the letters and magazines. Now, if only our furniture would arrive, so we could unpack our computer and e-mail everybody back home. Come to think of it, the four walls of our quarters were too quiet. I wouldn't mind the sound of a few TV sitcoms, either.

After Brad left for work the next day, I was certain I heard a dog barking nearby. With no TV set on, I was more aware of noises than usual. Except for the cars starting up in the early hours and the hourly city bus braking ahead of the corner stop, there were few disturbances to break my peace and quiet. Our curtains were tied back wide open, and I glanced out our front window—something I knew I was doing dozens of times a day, anyway. There were no dogs to be seen. Instead, I was treated to the spectacle of a sandy-haired soldier climbing down from a low balcony across the street, combat boots in hand. He landed on a row of petunias. The man with the unbuttoned camouflage shirt must have been What's-Her-Name's, new boy-toy. I'd really have fun telling Mom all our neighborhood news once we could connect.

Later, just as I was making myself a tuna sandwich for lunch, the dog sound repeated. Louder, more of a growl. Could a puppy have wandered in through a basement window and be locked inside? I raced out into the hallway—only to run into two very startled military policemen with a young German shepherd on a leash.

"Sorry to disturb you, ma'am. We didn't realize the building was occupied," the taller of the men said. The dog sat down, apparently content I didn't signify any sort of trouble.

I stared at the pair of soldiers. What in the world were they up to? They'd set up a portable table and two folding stools right in our hallway! Under the windowsill, I saw a chunky military radio in its give-away olive drab color, next to field binoculars.

They were spying! On somebody or on something. Neither corporal offered me anything in the way of an explanation, so I told them to have a nice day and closed my door. As an after-thought, I snapped on the chain lock.

If only I had a house telephone or a cell that functioned, my next reaction would have been to dial Brad at work. I unfolded the note paper where he'd scribbled his duty number. In all our time of living in Germany, I'd only used it once, when we ran out of coffee. I'd gone outside to the public telephone booth, inserted my coins and dialed. The neighbor-friends had mentioned all the other booths within a few-block radius were card telephones; and so far, I had no card. At the time, I rated figuring out a foreign phone as a significant milestone in my adjustment to our new locale.

Really, it was an insignificant step—a baby step. In truth, I hadn't dare venture far from our front porch. Call it fear of the unknown.

One morning, Anna-Maria had walked me to the corner bus stop and explained how to insert money into the automatic ticket machine, and she demonstrated how to punch the ticket buttons for the zones for downtown shopping, the zoo, and a couple of the American bases. Sooner or later, I was sure I'd board a bus and head somewhere. Until that happened, my mastering of the phone booth counted as my biggest feat.

I considered going outside, not to call Brad about picking something up at the commissary, but to inform him there was a major spy operation going on right under our noses—just outside our doorway. Sniffer-dog and all. I looked at my watch and decided to just wait it out. He was due home, soon.

I busied myself in our stack of forwarded mail. When Brad came home, he told me he knew all about the MPs and their mission. I didn't have to add a single detail. As he reminded me, the military world is a small one and personal secrets are hard to keep for long. Everyone pretty much knows everyone else's business.

The word around the battalion was it was a routine observation for contraband. "Some of our lovely neighbors across the way are dealing drugs, and I think the MPs are about to pounce on them!" Brad told me.

Who needed a television in this crazy place? We had it all: drug busts, lovers climbing out of windows, boozers, nudists, and gamblers. There was probably more, but we'd hadn't been around very long.

Brad suggested we sign up for the battalion's bowling league— mostly for me to meet more of the wives. After all, not everybody lived in our housing area. Brad was no big fan of bowling, but he was anticipating being sent on an extended training exercise, meaning he would spend three or four months in the field. He wanted me to have plenty of contacts so I wouldn't suffer from loneliness. Or boredom.

At the bowling alley, we finally met Sergeant Evander Lakeland in person. He gave us details about a free evening course in elementary German, and welcomed us to the unit. A real sportsman, he invited us on a weekend volksmarch—a fourteen-mile untimed hike, around the hills of Heidelberg. His sage advice was the worst thing anyone could do on any overseas assignment would be not to explore. He told us he could get us tickets to the upcoming German Grand Prix.

Things were looking up. Every Friday, Brad and I bowled. A couple times a week, I met neighbors for coffee and gossip. I'd added my name to the list to apply for several civil service jobs. Whenever we could, Brad and I would participate in volksmarches, and we were collecting quite a few prize medals from hiking around Deutschland.

Best of all, soon we'd have a telephone number to pass out to friends and family. One Monday, Brad came home to have lunch with me. Out of the blue. It was rare he could spare the time away from the unit. I greeted him with a longer-than-usual kiss, and he told me he had news. As I heated up some leftovers, I asked three times what it was.

He wouldn't say.

Just before he left to go back to work, he decided it was time to spill the beans.

"Hold onto your hat, we've got ourselves permanent quarters— with a large balcony!"

I giggled. I looked around the lifeless kitchen. Would I miss this dump? No way!

Brad slapped a folder down on the kitchen table. "Here you go," he said. "We finally have ourselves an address so our furniture can be delivered. We can move in next week. There's a phone, a back yard, all major appliances—"

"What about the neighbors?" I asked. "Are they all nuts?"

Brad laughed. "I think you know the answer to that. They're kooks, my darling, all kooks!"

THE END

LOVE & WAR

"Oops. I'm sorry, Major. Please, after you." I looked up into the bluest eyes I'd ever seen. He was tall, nearly as tall as Tyler, and he looked familiar. I couldn't place him, but I could tell by his sandy colored tan that he'd just returned from Iraq.

"Lt. Swain?" He asked.

I cocked an eyebrow. "Yes?" High heels and a red dress were hardly indicators of rank. How did he know me?

He held out a large hand. I clasped it in mine, and looked up at him, trying to read his eyes.

"I knew your husband," he said. "I'd know you anywhere. Tyler showed your photos around." I wanted to snatch my hand back and run from the room, but this man outranked me. Besides, something about him, the way he looked and the compassion in his face, made me want to stay by his side.

"Can we talk, Lieutenant? I wanted to speak with you today at the luncheon, but I couldn't catch your eye."

A deep sense of foreboding came over me. My eyes searched desperately for our hostess, my best friend Kelly. He finally released my hand. I put my martini down on the buffet table and nodded. Together we walked out of the house and onto the porch.

"I'm Sean, Sean Morganson," he said.

I gasped. Tyler had spoken about Sean. They were both with the 28th CASH, the Combat Support Hospital. Tyler said he was the best damn surgeon he'd seen in the field. He spoke of how he handled the Iraqi civilians. The doctors treated civilians and insurgents, but most wanted to give priority to their own guys. Tyler told me that Sean only wanted to be a healer. He didn't care about the politics or uniform of the injured.

The Major cleared his throat and looked away from me, into the middle distance towards the road. When he returned his gaze to me, his robin's egg blue eyes were soft. "I was with your husband when he died." He said. "His last words were, 'Tell Celia I love her. Tell her to live, live for both of us.' I wanted you to know. His last thoughts were of you."

I could see concern in his eyes. I felt hot tears run down my cheeks. I didn't know what to do. Nothing in military regulations covered crying in front of a Major. I wanted to run back inside, home, anywhere, but regulations did cover not leaving until dismissed. He reached up and gently caught my tears with his thumb.

"It's hard to go on, to be the one left behind. But it's a tribute to

Tyler," he said. "When you're ready, I'd like to take you to dinner. Tyler talked so much about you. I feel as if I know you."

I stumbled backward, and caught myself before I tumbled down the steps. I never expected someone from Tyler's unit to hit on me. True, Tyler died nearly a year ago. The gaping hole in my heart made it feel like yesterday. The Major's hand flashed out and caught me by the elbow. I felt a seam under my arm give way from the strain on the fabric. My cheeks burned with embarrassment and anger.

"Please," I sputtered, extremely uncomfortable and unable to vent to my anger. The small voice in my head reminded me of his rank. "Tell Kelly that I had to leave—an emergency. I'm sorry, I have to—"

"Lieutenant, I'm sorry. I was out of line. Please don't leave because of me. I, well, I only wanted to get to know you. I was offering friendship. I'm sorry. I understand how it sounded."

He looked so sad and confused. I was torn. I wanted to reach out and comfort him. I wanted to get away. I smiled what I hoped was a friendly smile instead of the grimace it felt like. He spoke before I could.

"I'm not much good with women. What I mean to say, and what I say, jumble up between my brain and mouth. Maybe that's why I'm a surgeon." He shrugged a bit and smiled. "Lousy bedside manner. If you're going to go, at least let me drive you home. You live on base?"

I chuckled, despite my discomfort. "Yes, but it will be a short drive." I pointed to a house not thirty feet away. "I live there."

He stood to attention. Like a West Point Cadet, he clicked his heels slightly, and offered me the crook of his arm. "Tyler went to the Point, didn't he?" Seeing my nod, he continued. "Well then, Lieutenant, I can promise you no PDA."

I couldn't help myself. I laughed out loud. "You know, since the dawn of the techno-information age, I haven't heard anyone refer to a public display of affection as PDA. I wonder what they call it at the Point these days." Chuckling to myself, I had a mental image of the long gray line emptying their pockets of their personal digital assistants and hoping not to crush them beneath their marching feet. "Talk about a language barrier!" I muttered.

Sean saw me to the door, watched me turn the key in the lock, and stayed on the porch as I closed the door in his face. He may have hoped for more. I wasn't ready to oblige.

I leaned my back against the rough wood panel and kicked off my heels. Clogs and scrubs were my usual uniform. My feet were killing me. Cramps snaked up my calves as my feet touched flat on the floor. I wanted to scream in pain. I remembered Tyler's touch. He'd rubbed my feet, and worked his way up to my leg muscles. He

23

had a gentle, healing touch. The cramps were nothing compared to the ache in my heart.

"Oh God," I whispered. "I'm not ready for this." I pulled the curtain aside, just a hair. I peeked out to the porch and the sidewalk beyond. Major Morganson's ramrod straight back headed to my neighbor's house to finish off the party.

Walking away from the window, I went into my kitchen, opened the refrigerator, and pulled out a chilled bottle of white wine. A surgical nurse, currently stationed at Womack Hospital, I normally didn't drink. My next shift wasn't for forty-eight hours. I was on leave, and since they knew the circumstances, I wasn't worried about an earlier call.

Taking the bottle and the glass, I padded into the bedroom on stocking feet. I slipped out of the red dress and looked at the damage. Unexpected tears stung my eyes when I saw the rip under the arm. It might be repairable, but I doubted I'd bother. I hung the dress up in the back of Tyler's closet. I rustled the arm of his dress uniform as I reached past. The smell of him assailed my nostrils. I tried to fight down the lump in my throat. After nearly a year, I still slept with his old sweaty T-shirt bunched in my fist. When he first left for Iraq, it was a comfort. After his death, it was a necessity. I turned, fighting back tears, and walked to the covered screened porch.

It had been a tough day. Tougher than I'd expected. Not as tough for me as Tyler's homecoming, though.

I curled up on the old chintz sofa we'd bought in a thrift store using some wedding money, poured myself a glass of wine, and let my mind wander back.

Last week, his unit went back to Ft. Bragg after a year in Iraq. I'd been rubbing that knowledge over in my mind for weeks before it happened. I knew I had to be at today's homecoming party. I not only owed it to Tyler and the men who'd served with him, I wanted to be there. I wanted to reassure them I didn't blame them. Tyler had died being Tyler. I would have expected nothing less.

I took a large sip of the wine, and grimaced as it bit down my throat. I saw myself again as I stopped at the door to the party room. I'd bought the low-cut but modest dress to welcome my husband home. I knew I looked great. Like I'd stepped out of a 1940's movie. My heels were high, and my heart was heavy. I'd taken a deep breath, straightened the skirt of my bright red sheath, pasted on a smile, squared my shoulders, put my hand on the door, and pushed it open.

The luncheon party had passed in a blur. I hugged everyone and accepted condolences. Celebrated life with the living and tried to stop looking for the one man I wanted to see more than any other.

The bright sun angled onto the porch interrupting my memories. I took another deep sip of the wine and rolled it over my tongue. I put the glass down, stood up, and walked to the kitchen for some cheese and crackers. I remembered the eerie feeling of someone watching me at the party. I couldn't pick anyone out. I'd thought, hoped, wished, it was Tyler's spirit. I could see him smiling, all six-feet-four of tall lean man, with a dusky desert tan like the rest of his group.

I didn't even have to close my eyes to feel his arm around me. Feel him tighten his grip around my waist and pull me towards him. It felt so real that I found myself glancing next to me, expecting to see him standing there. Now, I thought it was Sean Morganson whose gaze I'd felt. Mentally, I searched over the group of men and women gathered in the meeting room. Nope, I couldn't see Sean among them, but he must have been. He said he'd tried to catch my eye. I hadn't seen him until I got to Kelly's.

Kelly had followed up the general welcome home party with a party for the officers. I'd tried to beg off when she invited me, but she wheedled until I agreed to go.

I remembered Kelly's greeting at her door. She must have seen me coming up the walk.

"Here you go, kiddo." Kelly had said, and thrust one of her killer martinis into my hand "There's more vodka in here than vermouth." She winked. "It's stirred, not shaken." My friend studied me carefully, her brown eyes staring into mine. "You look like you need it. How are you feeling?"

My emotions were swirling around me. I didn't know how I felt, laughing one minute and fighting back tears the next. I took a sip and smiled my gratitude at her words. I mentally girded my loins, and decided to be the best guest she ever had. I tasted the drink again, a deep swallow this time. Kelly laughed when I said, "Excellent, you should have taken up anesthesia. Kelly, have you thought about a career in medicine?"

Her response was so typical, "Oh, la." She'd said in her New England accent. "It's just the southern belle in me, after all these years in Fayetteville!" Kelly laughed and wandered off in the direction of a lone woman standing near the front door.

I'd shaken my head in amusement and tipped my glass back again. This stuff could grow on you, I thought, as I wandered over to the buffet. That was when I'd bumped into Sean Morganson. "Make that Major Sean Morganson," I muttered to myself.

I certainly didn't run into him intentionally; I just wasn't paying attention. That was totally unlike me. I was always aware of my surroundings. How could I have missed him, twice? He was nearly as tall as Tyler. That meant he stood head and pretty much shoulders above everyone else. Yet I hadn't seen him, at Kelly's or at the welcome party. It didn't figure.

25

Feeling restless, I got up from the kitchen table and walked to the far side window. I wanted to shake the memories of today and bring myself back to the present.

I looked over at Kelly's house. The party was still in full swing. I wanted to get some information on Morganson. She might have it. I walked to the bookshelves that surrounded the fireplace in my living room. Our photo albums were there. I'd avoided them since Tyler's death.

I opened the book towards the back. I'd taken and sent a lot of photos over to him while he was gone. There were even some photos in the last letter—the one that returned, unopened. Still sealed, it fell out onto my lap now. I tucked it back into the album and flipped rapidly through the plastic sleeved pages. There it was. The group photo taken the day Tyler left. I got a magnifying glass from the end table drawer and studied the picture. Standing in the back, two men to the left of Tyler, was Sean Morganson. Funny, I hadn't remembered him. He must have been one of the doctors who rotated in to complete the staff. Thoughtfully, I closed the book.

"Ok, you were there, Major Morganson. How can someone as big as you be so invisible to me?" I spoke out loud, looked at my empty wine glass, and decided I'd had enough if I was talking to myself. I washed the glass and left it to dry in the drain board.

Going back to my bedroom, I pulled the red dress out of the closet and studied the rip under the arm again. Then throwing myself down on the bed, I gave way to the hurt I felt all day, sobbing great gasping sobs. I bought that dress to greet Tyler because I knew he'd love it. Instead, I'd worn it to greet his body coming home from Iraq. I figured the hell with what anyone thought. I'd bought the dress for Tyler. I was wearing it for Tyler. In the finest military tradition, no one had said a word, positive or negative. I could have shown up naked and the entire honor guard would have taken it in stride. Such is the Army.

I was startled awake by the telephone ringing. I must have fallen asleep while I was crying. Still clutching the soggy red dress, I fumbled for the telephone.

"Hello," I said. My voice sounded strange to my ears, as if I had a cold.

"Celia, it's Kelly. You okay? Sean told me about taking you home. I wanted to check on you. You sleeping?"

"Oh, Kelly, what time is it?" I fumbled for the clock on my night stand. Ten o'clock, early yet, and my lights were still on. "I must have fallen asleep." Then, as I grew more alert, I said, "Whoa, back up the pick up girl. Do you know Sean, I mean beyond his being with CASH?"

"Celia, don't be mad. Yes, he was with Tyler's group and he is with CASH, but he's also my brother-in-law. You know, the one I wanted you to meet. The one I told you about."

"Damn it, Kelly, and I told you no."

"Celia, calm down. I didn't plan this. I knew he knew Tyler, and I didn't plan this. In fact, I would have asked him to avoid you until you got used to the idea that Tyler's unit was back. I knew you weren't ready to meet him yet. Celia, believe me. I never suggested he talk to you. Not today."

Gulping down a sob, I said, "I'm sorry Kelly. I know I'm out of line. It's just, well, sometimes I feel like everyone is trying to fix me up. I'm not ready, not yet." I whispered. As I spoke, I was startled to feel a stirring of something in my heart. Like a little seed flowering. For the first time, I thought I might be ready. I wanted to get off the phone, to examine this new feeling.

"All right. I wanted to check on you, and Sean wanted to be sure that he hadn't upset you. Can I tell him you're okay?

"Huh? Oh. Yeah, you can tell him I'm fine. Has he been rotated here, or is he going back to his old base?"

"He'll be here. He's staying on at Womack. Thoracic Surgery. He'll be with Keith and me until housing is available."

Two days later, I walked into the nurse's coffee room at Womack. The good-looking new thoracic surgeon was on everyone's lips. One of my team members nearly went into raptures talking about how wonderful he was to work with and what a marvelous surgeon he was.

"Ok, Corey, who is this paragon of manhood and surgery?" I asked with a chuckle. I'd never heard this group be so impressed. Generally, we liked our surgeons, some more than others, but this—if the guy asked for volunteers, he'd better step back—this crowd would stampede.

"New guy, he was with Tyler's unit in Iraq. Dr. Morganson. Did you see him at the homecoming?"

The duty chart I was holding slipped from my bloodless fingers. "Sean Morganson?" I asked very slowly, drawing out each word. Mentally I smacked my forehead with the heel of my hand. How dumb could I be? Of course I'd be working with him. I was a surgical nurse and I worked the thoracic unit. I must have been in la la land!

"You'll love him. Scuttlebutt has it he's single, and I think he's got family here on base." Corey waggled her hand back and forth at me. "You're not interested in him that way. He'll probably request you for every surgery. You'll be the only one not making goo goo eyes at him!" Corey shook her head when I made a face. "Celia, we're all here for you. You know that. Are you ready to be back today?" She asked gently.

Picking up the duty roster again, I checked down the surgeries assigned to my name. Yep, there it was. Our first surgery would be in an hour. My first of the day. "Well, I guess I'd better be," I replied to Corey. "My first dance is in an hour. Any quirks on how he likes the circulator to set his tray? Any preferences in style or routine?" I was trying to bring the conversation back to the professional. I didn't want to dwell on the little trill I'd felt in my stomach when I saw my name next to his.

He scrubbed in before I arrived. That bothered me. It was part of my duty as surgical nurse to help him scrub. I wasn't late, but the other nurses hadn't warned me that he was extra early. I saw his blue eyes crinkle over his mask when he saw me, and I felt my heart flutter again.

"Hi Celia, I was glad to see we'd finally be working together. I just finished another patient and scrubbed in instead of getting coffee." He looked through the square window to the operating theater. "Looks like we're ready when you are. Pete, the anesthesiologist, just nodded over to me; the patient is ready."

I scrubbed in and changed into the gown, hat, booties, gloves, and mask. The other nurses were right. This man had magic hands. I watched in awe as his long fingers wielded the scalpel with a ballerina's precision. Every time his blue eyes met mine over the mask, I felt a quick flutter. The only misstep was at the end of the surgery. I reached over, ready to close for him as I did for so many other surgeons. He shook his head gently and said, "I'll do it Celia."

We stripped off our gloves and dropped them into the waiting trash cans. He looked at me and said, "We work well together. I felt you were anticipating my every request."

Smiling my thanks, I said, "Yes, all except at the end. I'm sorry, Doctor. . ."

"No need to be. I've heard you have a fine stitch in closing patients. That's something to be proud of. I guess, from my time in the field, I use closing the patient as a decompression of sorts. This one is done, the next not started." Laughing he said, "That sounds so Zen. Habit, really. I'm sure once I'm more accustomed to homeland surgery again, you'll be closing for me too." He started to leave the scrub room, stopped in mid-stride, turned, and said, "Celia, I understand you don't want a dinner just yet, but how about a cup of coffee?"

My heart fluttered again. My first instinct was to say no. This time it wasn't because I wasn't ready, but because I was afraid I might be. He must have seen the confusion on my face. He cocked his head to the side and said, "Oh, I see. I'm sorry. I didn't think." He turned again and started to walk away.

I hesitated a second before I hurried to catch up with him. "Doctor, if the invitation is still open, I'd love a caffeine fix."

My heart melted when he smiled and nodded.

Both of us were careful to keep the conversation on neutral topics. We talked about Kelly, her husband Keith, Fayetteville, and the nearby Carolina coast. Both of us loved the water and scuba diving. He added horseback riding into the mix. I opened my mouth to tell him I'd love to have dinner with him, when the hissing vibration of his beeper cut me short.

"Damn," he said. "It's an emergency. I was hoping the schedule would stand. You want to scrub in?"

I shook my head. "Would love to, but I can't. I'm scheduled for a two o'clock."

I noticed how straight his back was when he walked away. He was all military. It was second nature.

When I got home, there was a message light flashing on my machine. I picked up the telephone handset and looked at the caller ID number. I didn't recognize it. I put the phone back on the base, punched in the numbers for voice mail, and sorted through my paper mail waiting for the message to play. When I heard Sean's voice come over the speaker, I dropped the mail. I'd been thinking about his dinner invitation all afternoon. I'd been ready to tell him I'd love to go when his beeper sounded. Now here he was, on my phone, asking me to call.

I hadn't dated anyone since Tyler's death. We'd met in the army. We knew the risks, but we loved the life. I'd done a combat tour in 2003. As a nurse with a surgical major, I'd expected it. We'd joked that I'd be the only one with combat tales. Tyler's tour came later. We'd talked about what would happen if one of us died. We agreed we each wanted the other to find someone else. We just didn't know how hard that would be. When Tyler died, I thought a part of me died with him. The part that wanted to share my life with anyone ever again.

I stared at the phone for a good ten minutes, running the thought of a date over in my mind, the way I'd run my tongue over a sore tooth. It still hurt, but not quite as badly. Wait a minute. He hasn't asked me out, not yet, and he didn't ask me out at Kelly's. All he said was he would like to take me to dinner. I'm the one who's rushing, I thought to myself as I scooped up the mail from the floor. I picked up the handset, put the phone on the table and the mail to my ear. I laughed when I realized what I'd done and decided to have some dinner before I called him back. If I couldn't figure out how to make a call, I probably wasn't ready to make it.

I moved to the kitchen and began to prepare a steak and salad for dinner. I remembered a conversation I had with Kelly. It bordered on an argument. She'd wanted to fix me up with Keith's brother when he got back from Iraq. Little did I know then, her intended blind date was with Sean, but I yelled at her for making the suggestion because I didn't want to date.

In my mind's eye, I could see what Tyler's broken body must have looked like when he'd thrown himself on that IED. Part of what CASH was about was getting surgeons to the wounded wherever they were. Tyler was part of a group of surgeons going to a battle sight in town. Their job was to field treat casualties too severe for transport. Tyler had seen and identified the bomb, and he'd saved lives at the expense of his own. Typical Tyler. So were the words Sean brought me from that day: "Go on with your life; live your life for us both."

Tyler and I had discussed it, and now it was Tyler's last wish. Suddenly that felt like more responsibility than I could take on. How could I live my life for both of us? I didn't know what our life together would bring. Our life together would always be an unfinished song, a dream. I couldn't tell myself what he would want. The only thing I could actually know is what I want. "Darn, it's not fair. How am I supposed to make these decisions alone? Tyler, help me here!" I prayed aloud. "I don't know what to do. When I lost my parents, no one urged me to find a new pair. I've lost my husband. Why is everyone trying to get me to find a new one? Why am I thinking I might like to feel myself in a man's arms again? Oh, God, you know I loved Tyler. Does this desire mean I didn't?"

The partially grilled steak lost its appeal. I took it off the skillet and dropped it into the garbage. The salad I'd made followed. I hadn't felt this bad since Tyler first died. I couldn't stop the questions. They piled on fast and furious. Did I love him enough? If I dated, was I betraying him? Was I running ahead of myself? I shook my head. If these issues didn't come up with Sean, they'd come up with someone else. The problem was, I was alive. I felt guilty about truly living. Most of my friends encouraged me to look to the cute Captains I worked beside as part of my surgical nurse duties. A lot of the cute Captains had suggested the same.

They just didn't get it. Anyone I met here could end up just like Tyler. Blown to bits. For all I knew, so could I. Most lifers did more than one combat tour in wartime. Sean was a lifer, too.

I wandered back into the living room, sat on the couch, and stared out the front window. Base life went on at its usual pace. Nothing stopped for me, or for my tragedy. I wished we'd had children. I sighed deeply and dropped my head backwards onto the back of the couch. Tyler used to laugh at me when I did that. He warned me I'd give myself whiplash one of these days. I smiled at the memory and let my mind drift, half listening to the night noises outside my open windows.

I woke with a start, my head jerking upright from the couch-back. I saw a man's shape in front of me. I tried to force myself off the couch, but I couldn't move. I tossed my head from side to side. I opened my mouth. Nothing came out. In that moment, I knew I was sleeping, but somehow I felt awake. I was petrified, but also comforted. Whatever was in front of me, it meant me no harm. "Celia." The shape said softly. I could see it was a man's shape. I couldn't see features. "Sean's a good man. Celia, he was there. He knows. Celia, don't die with me. What's the point? Please, Celia, listen."

The voice faded on the last words and the shape—Tyler's shape, I realized—disappeared. I looked at my hand and saw it move. I curled each of my fingers in turn, and felt my short nails bite into my palm. When did I wake up? Had Tyler been here? Was I awake when he came? I turned my head to the window. The curtains blew in on the gentle breeze, the night noises had stopped. I could hear the crickets chirp and the sound of a distant motor. Turning away from the window, I looked at the clock. It was three in the morning. I got up and went into the kitchen to make myself a cup of tea. Glancing out the window, I saw Kelly's kitchen light still on. I could just make out a male shape sitting at her kitchen table. The silver hair told me it was Sean.

I glanced at my face reflected back to me in the glass front of the microwave. I patted my hair, and glanced back at the man in Kelly's house. I knew he was waiting for his base housing to open up. In the meantime, he was staying with the Bradleys. Idly, I wondered where he'd called from. The caller ID number hadn't been Kelly's, or the hospital's.

I opened a cupboard. The kettle was whistling merrily as the water boiled. I reached back behind the mugs and plates and grabbed a ceramic teapot shaped like a round General. Tyler and I had bought it on our honeymoon. We'd gone to St. Thomas in the Virgin Islands and found it sitting on a shelf in a tourist shop. He seemed so out of place and so right for us. We called him General Polly, as in Rolly Polly. I'd put him away when Tyler died. The sight of him tore at my heart. Now I pulled him out, rinsed him in hot water, and quickly tossed in five spoons of loose tea.

Halfway to Kelly's, I nearly lost my nerve. What was I thinking, taking tea to a man I hardly knew, and at this hour of the morning? For all I knew he was on his way to the hospital for some emergency. Kelly and Keith certainly didn't keep these hours. I nearly turned around, but then I felt a gentle shove in the small of my back.

Glancing over my shoulder, I mouthed a "thank you" to Tyler and continued on my way. Mounting the kitchen steps, I tapped softly

31

on the door. I could see the tiredness in his face, and I wondered again if I was doing the right thing. Sean rose and came to the door. Pulling aside the curtain, he saw me. I watched his mouth open into a wide grin, and I saw some of the tiredness drop from his face.

"I was just thinking about you," he said as he took my arm and led me to the table. "I saw the light when I got up, but I didn't know if you were awake or not. The tea smells great."

"I was thinking about you too. Any word on your quarters?" I went to the cupboard, got two cups and saucers, and brought them back to the table.

"Wednesday, no sooner. I sold everything before I left Benning for Iraq. I didn't want any reminders. Celia, we have to talk. Maybe now isn't the time." Sean removed the strainer from his cup and placed it on his saucer. I watched as he slowly stirred sugar into the steaming liquid. I felt my stomach clench. I wasn't sure whether I should stay or run. His slight smile told me he must have read the look on my face. "It's not that bad," he whispered. His long fingers reached up and grazed my cheek, following the line of my face to my jaw and stopping under my chin.

I couldn't help myself. I trembled. My own emotions confused me. I wanted to throw myself into his arms. I wanted to run. His touch ignited a fire in me I thought was dead. "Sean. . ." I began.

"No, Celia, don't interrupt. I want to tell you. I know how you feel, and I know how hard it is for you right now."

I reached up my hand and put a finger on his lips to silence him. I could see tears welling, and I didn't want to hear whatever he had to tell me. Not now, not when I'd finally decided I was ready.

He kissed my fingers and rotated his hand to grasp mine in his. "I lost my wife. It was before I went to Iraq, not too much before. Close enough so that going to a combat zone seemed like, well. . ." He signed deeply and stared out the window. He couldn't see anything, not with the kitchen lights on, but he continued to stare. "I thought it was a wonderful opportunity to die. I didn't expect to come back."

"Sean, don't. There's no reason to tell me this. You don't have to. Not now, maybe not ever." I wasn't sure what he was going to say next. I knew, somehow, that it was going to change my life.

He twined his fingers with mine and lifted my hand to his lips. Gently kissing my fingertips he smiled and said, "Tyler saved my life. Tyler, he was my best friend in CASH. You were all he talked about. No matter what was going on, you were on his mind. You were in every conversation. I envied him. My God, how I envied him. When he died, right in front of me, I wished it had been me. It should have been me. For a long time, I wanted it to be me. When I met you, I saw how devastated you still were. I wished it had been me all over again.

32

Then I was glad it wasn't. Tyler wanted you to go on with your life. Celia, he really did."

I felt a weight drop from my heart. For the first time since the Chaplain knocked at my door, I felt serene. I knew what Tyler wanted, and I knew what I wanted and needed.

His blue eyes bore into mine. I felt like he was seeing the back of my soul.

"I know," I whispered, "we'd talked about it before I went to Afghanistan and before he went to Iraq. We both wanted it. Only it's easier when you talk about it and you think you're the one not coming back. You never think that you might be the one who has to get on with living. I know what Tyler wanted. And Sean, I think I'm ready now. If you are."

He was out of the kitchen chair like a shot. I felt him enfold me in his arms and hug me to him. I heard him whisper into my hair but I couldn't make out the words. I was too busy listening to an inner voice, one I recognized as Tyler's, cheering me on.

THE END

A SOLDIER'S WIFE CAN HANDLE ANYTHING
Even when she fears the worst

I hurried to the mailbox and pulled open the door. With trembling fingers I sorted through the stack of mail—

Nothing from Jason.

Again.

Four weeks now and not a word.

I reminded myself that it didn't mean anything. Mail out of Iraq is impossible to predict. In his letters, Jason said mine sometimes took nearly a month to get to him.

But four weeks without hearing from him. . . . I swallowed my tears and headed back into the apartment—a lonely place without my beloved husband.

I met Jason Hennessey at the candle-making plant where we both worked. It was the kind of dead-end job that everybody talked about leaving behind for better things. The only problem was that many of our coworkers had been there for more than thirty years. I took some college courses off and on for two years, but I couldn't afford to become a full-time student. My mother was working on her third husband and my dad had little contact with my two sisters and me ever since he and Mom divorced when I was eight. With no one to help pay for college or encourage me along, my attendance was sporadic.

Jason laughed at my efforts and said he wasn't "college material." But he didn't want to work at the candle factory for the rest of his life, either. We talked a lot during our breaks and I was almost surprised the first time he asked me out. He was handsome and funny and all the women there wanted his attention; I couldn't figure out what he saw in me.

"You're not like the other girls I know, Robin," he said when I asked him about it on our second date. "All they care about is having a good time and spending their paychecks as fast as they earn them."

"I thought guys like girls who only want to have a good time," I said teasingly.

He grew serious. "Not me. I don't plan on being here my whole life and I want a woman who isn't satisfied with settling, either."

That night when I got home I thought about what he said. I never gave it much thought before, but I knew he was right: I didn't want to settle for what life pushed at me just because it was easier

34

than fighting for what I wanted. So that night I decided I would get a college degree even if it took me ten years to earn it, and that I wouldn't marry the first guy who offered me a warm bed to crawl into like my mother did. I would wait for the man of my dreams and I would have children someday—a whole houseful—and I would teach them to believe in God and in themselves.

In no time at all Jason and I were dating exclusively. Both of us wanted to save money so we kept our dates simple. He had his own apartment while I still lived with my mom and sisters even though I was twenty-one. For most of our dates, we rented movies and ordered pizza and spent the evening at his apartment. Sometimes we played cards. When things got too hot-and-heavy one night, I told him I wanted to wait for sex until after I was married.

Jason was surprised by my confession, but he didn't ridicule me. "I'm sorry, Robin—I didn't know you felt that way."

"I know—I should've told you sooner. You see, I wasn't exactly raised to honor chastity, but I've seen what falling for the wrong guy can do to a woman."

"Do you think I'm the wrong guy?"

"No, that's not what I meant. But the truth is I only want to give myself to one man. And even then, I want it to happen on my wedding night. It's very important to me, Jason, that I save myself for him, whoever he is." I blushed and ducked my head. "I guess that sounds really old-fashioned and anti-feminist, huh?"

He put his hand on my chin and tilted my head up that our eyes met. "On the contrary, it's about the sexiest thing I've ever heard."

Our eyes held for a long moment and then he dropped his hand. "I respect you, Robin, and I promise you that I won't do anything that might make you want to compromise your beliefs."

At that moment I knew I was in love with him. In case he didn't feel the same way about me, I decided to limit my time alone with him. I knew I couldn't guarantee that I would be able to hold onto my commitments, even if he were a true gentleman.

All my worry was in vain. A month later Jason surprised me with an engagement ring. "I can't offer you an easy life, Robin," he said when he opened the box and held it out to me, "but I can offer you my undying love. I want to make you happy. I want to tuck you into bed every night and wake up beside you every morning. Marry me, Robin, and I promise to love you for the rest of my life."

I slid off the couch and into his arms, my face streaked with tears. My mother was ecstatic; I think she was actually a little relieved that I would be moving out, but I also think she could see that Jason truly loved me, and that just maybe I'd found the fulfillment she'd been searching for her whole life.

After just a few weeks of married bliss in Jason's too-small apartment, he brought home some Army recruitment pamphlets. "I've been thinking about this for a long time," he told me earnestly. "If you don't like the idea, I'll throw them away and we'll never talk about it again. But if you think it's something we should consider, I'd like to look these over with you."

My heart caught in my throat when I looked at the stern-looking soldier on the front cover of one of the pamphlets. Pride for my country swelled up inside of me at the thought of my husband dressed in one of those uniforms, defending his country, but then I realized that my husband of only three weeks would have to leave for basic training if he enlisted, and I couldn't go with him. And then I wondered, What would happen if our country went to war and something happened to him? I couldn't bear the thought of living without Jason.

"Let me think about it while we fix dinner," I told him.

He kissed me and smiled. "Thanks, honey. I love you."

We puttered around our tiny galley kitchen, bumping into each other while he peeled potatoes and I browned a pound of hamburger. All the while I imagined the babies I wanted to have. Certainly, I realized, the military would pay all of my medical bills. As it was, the insurance I had through the candle factory would barely pay seventy percent—and even then, only after an ungodly deductible had been paid. And what about childcare? I certainly couldn't afford to stay at home with my babies like I dreamed of doing. On the other hand, the military would make it possible for Jason and me to get out of our tiny apartment and maybe actually see some of the world. All of a sudden I started imagining what it would be like to live in Europe or even Japan. I had never been out of the Midwest and the thought of seeing the world with the man I loved was exciting, I'll admit.

I turned off the flame under the skillet and turned to face Jason. "Okay, Jason," I said. "Let's do it."

His eyes widened. "You mean it? Just like that?"

"Sure. On one condition." I put the spatula on the counter and paused for effect. "As long as you promise to let me decide how many babies we have."

He dropped a half-peeled potato into the pan, wrapped his arms around me, and lifted me off the floor. "One or a dozen, baby—it doesn't matter to me as long as you promise me that they'll all be as beautiful as you are." He set me back on the floor and gazed into my eyes. "But you've got to promise me something else, too—that no matter how many kids we have, you'll keep working on your degree."

"Agreed."

We waited until after the holidays were over before Jason signed up. That February he was sent to Fort Dix in New Jersey. Then every

36

night after work I came home to our tiny, lonesome apartment and cried and wrote page after page of letters to him telling him how much I loved him and that I couldn't wait to see him again. I didn't tell him how hard the waiting was for me because he already knew. Eight weeks later, Mom and my stepdad, Carl, drove me to New Jersey to see Jason graduate. I was never so proud. Unfortunately he was sent directly to Indiana for his specialized training so we only had one afternoon together. At least Indiana made visits a lot more feasible. We even hoped he would occasionally get weekend passes so we could meet somewhere in the middle.

During Jason's first weekend pass a month later we met in Springfield, Illinois. Two weeks later I wrote and told him that I was pregnant. Soon afterward, I let the apartment go and moved back home with my mom and stepdad. Jason came home for a month after training and then I joined him in California. I was thrilled; I was back with the man I love, his child was growing inside of me, and he had a wonderful assignment. We were both hoping for overseas duty, but we also knew he had plenty of time for that. Still, all of our new military friends told us not to get too "cozy" in California.

Early on the morning of September 11, I heard Jason cry out from the bathroom. He was due to leave for work in another fifteen minutes or so and was shaving while the radio played beside him. He had the volume turned down low so he wouldn't disturb me; I'd just entered my second trimester and I wasn't sleeping well.

"Jason?" I called out, sitting up in bed and looking around. "What's the matter?"

He threw open the bathroom door and charged into the bedroom. His face was still wet and his uniform shirt was unbuttoned and the expression in his eyes scared me. "Get up," he shouted, scaring me even more. He ran through the bedroom and down the stairs without waiting for me. "Come on—hurry up," he called over his shoulder. "We've been attacked."

I stumbled out of bed with my heart pounding, frantically wondering, What is he talking about? Attacked? By whom? By the time I got to the living room he had the TV on and he was clicking the remote to find CNN. Then suddenly, like a waking nightmare of the worst kind—there it was in living color: One of the World Trade Center towers was on fire and a plane had just crashed into the other one.

My mind still wouldn't register what was happening. "Jason, what's going on?"

He turned away from the TV and looked at me. Real fear welled inside of me at the look on my strong husband's face—a look of confusion, anger, and a kind of determination I'd never seen before.

My voice broke. "Jason? What is it? What's happening?"

He came to me and we held each other while we watched the news broadcast. It was on every channel. The President was in Florida and was on his way to a secured location. No one knew where the vice president was. There was word out of Washington that an attack had been made on the Pentagon. The country was in turmoil. I buried my face in Jason's unbuttoned shirt and wept. He only allowed me a few minutes of grief.

"I've got to go, Robin," he said, glancing at the clock behind me on our living room wall.

"No!" I gasped, clutching his shirt. "Don't leave me—not today—not now!"

"Honey, I've got to. I'll call you as soon as I get there. Stay inside. Watch the news coverage and wait for my call."

On that terrible day, like the rest of America, neither one of us knew what the next twenty-four hours would bring. Indeed, for the next few days, no one at the base knew what to expect from one moment to the next. We were all gravely concerned that the country would be attacked again and certainly, we knew that military installations would be prime targets. The local churches held candlelight vigils and all of the husbands and wives of the soldiers consoled each other the best we could. I finally got hold of my mother back home.

"Come home, Robin," she pleaded into the phone, crying. "It's too dangerous there!"

"It's dangerous everywhere now, Mom."

"Oh, honey, I know, but I just hate the thought of one of my babies not being here with me, by my side!"

As an expectant mother, I knew how she felt. But I also knew I couldn't leave Jason.

The next few days I joined my fellow Americans sitting in front of the television, reading off the names of those missing or dead from the attacks. I was numb; I didn't want to go anywhere or do anything. Even though I didn't recognize any of the names scrolling across the bottom of my TV screen, I couldn't stop mourning for those people—innocent victims going to work on just another Tuesday morning, and suddenly their lives were stolen from them for no good reason at all.

All anyone talked about was war against Afghanistan. Like everyone else, I wanted blood. I wanted vengeance. But at the same time, I knew war could very well mean that my husband would be in danger. My greatest fear was that he would be shipped to Afghanistan or another of the hotbeds and be killed there and never come home to me.

Lord, don't let them take Jason, I prayed constantly.

Jason, on the other hand, wanted nothing more than to launch an attack himself. He took the attacks on the World Trade Center and the Pentagon personally. He wanted to be the one to capture Osama Bin Laden and bring his head home on a stake.

After what seemed like a lifetime of waiting and fretting, President Bush finally gave Afghanistan an ultimatum. The next morning Jason's engineering unit was given their orders: They were to leave on an undisclosed date in the near future to an undisclosed location. We all assumed it was the Middle East, but we weren't supposed to discuss it. No one had to tell us that; as it was, we didn't want to talk about it.

The night before Jason left I fixed his favorite dinner and set the table with our best dishes, the ones his aunt gave us at our wedding. Neither of us had much of an appetite, at least not for food. After we'd nibbled at our food with me barely able to hold my tears in check, Jason said the dishes could wait and picked me up and carried me upstairs to our bedroom. Within moments my best dress was in a wrinkled heap on the floor and for a little while, at least, Jason and I helped each other forget about what the future would—and could—bring.

Later, he propped himself up on one elbow beside me in our marriage bed and traced my chin and neck with one fingertip. "I want you to do something for me while I'm gone, Robin," he said softly.

Tears sprang to my eyes. I didn't want to think about him going anywhere and I couldn't even answer him.

"Robin? Are you listening?"

I swallowed hard and nodded. "I'm listening. Anything you want, Jason, I'll do it."

"Good, because I want you to enroll in some college courses."

I stared at him. "Not now. I'm going to have our baby, Jason."

"In five months. In the meantime, you've got time to take a few classes. And don't say that we can't afford it; they're giving steep discounts to military families right now. I don't want you to sit around this apartment and mope the whole time I'm away; you're too smart for that. Now, will you promise me?"

I didn't want to sit around and mope, either. I was terrified of that happening, actually. "If you really want me to."

He leaned down and kissed me. "I really want you to, Robin. After the baby comes, you won't have any time to yourself. You need to take advantage of this opportunity while you still can."

We made love again and then Jason fell asleep in my arms. I lay there looking at him and listening to him breathe and I couldn't believe how much I loved him. I put my hand on my rounded belly and felt for the baby's movement. At least while Jason was gone I would still have a part of him with me at all times, right under my heart.

Two weeks after Jason left I walked onto the state university campus feeling like a big, fat fish out of water. I started taking classes, studied diligently, and wrote letters to Jason nearly every single day even though I didn't know for sure where he was stationed. As it was, I knew he probably wouldn't receive half of them. The letters I received from him were sporadic. He always asked about the baby and came up with crazy, off-the-wall baby names to cheer me up, but he never mentioned his location or his assignment. In fact, reading his letters, I could almost believe that he was back at Fort Dix, and for all I really knew—maybe he was.

I loved my English composition class; in fact, I almost hated to see the semester end. But I had the baby to look forward to; I busied myself with sewing curtains in shades of yellow and green and I bought a layette for the other bedroom in our little apartment. I tried to stay busy. Hopefully Jason would be home soon and I could think about continuing my education then. As it was, my days were filled with homework, poring over baby books and magazines, and waiting for letters from Jason. Thankfully, I developed a close relationship with another Army wife who was also a newlywed. Carrie and her husband, Derek, were originally from Seattle. Like me, Carrie was getting little word from her husband, so the two of us spent a lot of time together. She had a six-month-old daughter, Zoë, and I learned a lot about babies just from spending time in her apartment.

Then on the tenth of February, my water broke while I was at home in my apartment. I called Carrie and she rushed right over; it was a Sunday and she was able to find another friend to keep Zoë for her while she took me to the hospital. The only thing that marred my blessed event was the fact that Jason wasn't there to see our Jessica Elizabeth brought into the world.

What a surprise I got two weeks later. We spouses always heard when shipments of soldiers were coming home, especially if there were any men and women from our base on board. This time, though, because I was so preoccupied and busy with getting accustomed to being a new mother, I didn't hear the news, but Carrie knew all about it and she insisted that I go along with her to meet the returning troops. Let me tell you—I sure wasn't prepared when Jason himself stepped off that ship! Our little reunion was even captured on film by a national newspaper; I guess the photographer couldn't resist snapping a few shots of a returning hero being welcomed home by his wife and two-week-old daughter.

For the next year, Jason remained stateside. Apparently, I have no trouble conceiving because Jessie was barely pulling herself up to a standing position by the time I discovered that I was expecting again. I only prayed that the baby would come before Jason was shipped out again. As it was, we both watched the coverage of Iraq with mounting anxiety. Surely, I reasoned, he won't have to go there when he just returned from Afghanistan. But I held my breath every time I heard some news report on Iraq. I knew that Jason was anxious, too, but he wouldn't discuss it with me. Then we got word.

Jason's unit was shipping out again.

Not again, I thought, feeling like my heart would break from the news. At the time, I was nearly eight months along and facing another delivery without my husband at my side. Jason took Lamaze classes with me and we were so looking forward to having this baby together, but it wasn't to be and as the realization dawned on me that he was going to war and leaving us again, I couldn't stop crying and saying a lot of things I later regretted. But such is the life of a military spouse. I accepted this—or at least, I tried to. In fact, it was rare that a soldier would serve in both Afghanistan and Iraq, but Jason's unit was bucking the odds and at an undetermined time on an undisclosed date he would leave us again. Then one afternoon while we were in the car on our way home from a prenatal visit with my ob/gyn, Jason's cell phone rang. Instantly, my heart sank; his cell phone calls were almost always work related. Indeed, we found out right then that he had two days before he shipped out.

Another few weeks and our baby would've been born, I thought miserably. For weeks after he left, I was so depressed that I didn't want to talk to anyone.

In the beginning, Jason's letters and phone calls came regularly, considering the way things work nowadays in the Army. He was even on the other end of a conference call during the delivery of our second daughter, Amber Rose. Gradually, though, his calls became less and less frequent until it seemed like all I was doing was walking to and from our mailbox and waiting for word from him.

My depression grew, festering deep inside of me like a black, terrible thing. Amber was a colicky baby and much more temperamental than Jessie. Or maybe I'm the one who was temperamental. I'd aced two classes at the state university and I knew that going back for another semester would do wonders for my mood, but I also knew that I couldn't afford to pay for classes and a babysitter, so I faced a vexing dilemma.

The solution came to me in the form of my father, whom I hadn't seen in two years. My sister told him that I was living in Southern California and he paid me a visit while he was passing through; Dad sells computer programs to companies and I happened to be living in his territory. Considering our rocky past, we actually had a wonderful visit. He loved meeting his granddaughters and he even admitted to me that he knew he'd never exactly been the greatest father.

"I'll be working out here for the foreseeable future, though," he said, "and I'd really like to visit again, if you'll have me."

True to his word, he invited me to dinner two weeks later. He paid for a sitter for Jessie and Amber and the two of us dined at a fashionable East Indian restaurant. Over dinner, when I told him of my desire to continue my studies, he offered to help with the tuition. I almost refused, after all, where was he when my sisters and I were growing up? But before I could say no, I realized it was my pride talking. Fathers help their children through school all the time and I decided then and there that if he really wanted to pay, I would gladly let him.

I'd registered for three classes before I heard from Jason again. I actually began to wonder if it was possible that I would complete my degree and graduate before I could even tell him what I was doing. Regardless, with Dad picking up the tab for everything except a sitter, I reentered the collegiate world.

Thankfully, my busy home life as a mom of two little ones going it alone, topped with my grueling study schedule, cured my depression. At least for five hours a day, four days a week, I got out of our apartment and found something to do with my mind besides mothering and dwelling on how much I missed my husband. And I wasn't the only one on campus in my situation; I found other young mothers I could relate to from the very first day of classes and we shared lunches in the student union, baby pictures, and war stories. Surprising to me, there were even men in our newfound "clique" who missed their enlisted wives every bit as achingly as we missed our husbands. Oh, we were a sad little group, all right, but we drew strength from one another.

Then one Thursday I had an hour between my last two classes of the day. It was too inconvenient and too much of a trek to drive all the way home in between so I usually spent that hour in the library or in the park, reading.

Late that Thursday afternoon, I logged onto the Internet using the library's computer to see if I could find out any news about recent developments in Iraq. Thankfully, with the war on, there are all kinds of sites online nowadays where people like me can get in touch with other spouses who are also trying to keep abreast of the war situation and where our mates are. Much of the actual, factual information is classified and known only to the "need-to-knows" of the military, so nearly everything exchanged on the websites is hearsay. Still, it makes us all feel like we are at least connected to our loved ones in some small way.

On this particular day, the online rumors were all about an engineering company that had been ambushed in the last twelve hours. Immediately as I scrolled through the posts, reading furiously, my heart sank and my mind started to race with mounting fear. I had to remind myself repeatedly that all the information was was rumors, and probably little more, just so I wouldn't feel like I was going to die right in front of that computer.

And just remember—Jason's unit isn't the only engineering unit over there, I told myself over and over again.

Still, I surfed the web until it was time to leave for my next class, trying to find something—anything—that would let me know if the story were true or not. None of the news sites mentioned anything about an ambush, but then again—they only know what the military wants them to know.

Needless to say, I didn't get much out of my last class that day.

As soon as I got home I called Carrie. She brought her little girl over and we ordered pizza for dinner. With Amber in the playpen and Jessie and Zoë absorbed with playing Barbies on the floor in front of us in my living room, Carrie and I took turns commanding the remote and flipping from one news program to another.

"I'm sure the fact that we're not finding anything on the news means there was no ambush," Carrie assured me over and over. "They're always reporting whenever a plane is shot down or someone's taken hostage. You shouldn't go on those websites, Robin; they're too upsetting."

I nodded. "I know, but I want to know what's happening with Jason."

"We aren't supposed to know, Robin—haven't you realized that by now? All we can do is pray and hope that our husbands are safe and sound."

Easy for her to say. Her husband is a supply sergeant and she knew where he was all the time.

I woke up early the next morning and went straight for the TV. It was all over the news—an engineering battalion had been ambushed near a small town in northern Iraq. They were not giving any "specific information" at that time.

I switched off the TV and cried until I heard Amber upstairs fussing for her breakfast. Fortunately, I didn't have any classes that day and my Fridays were usually spent running errands and shopping. That day, though, I didn't even want to leave the apartment. I wanted to sit glued to the TV and all I could think was: What if Jason calls? What if the Army tries to notify me? I did a little housekeeping and a few loads of laundry. Amber was fussy and wanted me to hold her all day. Jessie was cranky, too, because I didn't take her out to lunch at McDonald's, which was our usual Friday routine.

Carrie came over after the girls went down for their naps. "I know you're worried, Robin," she said, "but don't be. If it involved Jason, you'll be notified."

She said it to make me feel better but after that, every time the phone rang my heart skipped a beat. I guess you could say that's when I finally realized that I'm just not cut out to be a soldier's wife.

I slept fitfully that night and woke early on Saturday. The news coverage over the weekend was minimal; I guess if you get shot on a Saturday, your family doesn't hear the details until a regular working day. By Monday, news of the ambush had all but disappeared from my TV screen. I was beginning to think I'd imagined the whole thing.

Against Carrie's advice, I went back to the Internet. The chat rooms I visited were full of people speculating on what happened. Many blamed President Bush. Many blamed the military for not letting the American people know what was going on. I didn't know what to think—I just wanted to hear my husband's voice and know for certain that he was still alive.

I was tempted to stay home from class so I could maintain my presence in the various chat rooms, but I didn't. The babysitter came to my apartment so I knew she would be home to take a message if Jason or anyone from the Army called. Nevertheless, I hurried home from classes all that week, expecting to hear that Jason had called. Every day my babysitter, Wendi, met me at the door with the same sad, apologetic look.

By the end of that week I was desperate for any news from my husband. I have to honestly admit to you that at that point, I almost would have welcomed even bad news. At least then, I would know more than I did—which means more than absolutely nothing.

One evening I put Amber down for the night and brought Jessie downstairs with me to read to her. She was two and a half then and very bright for her age—at least, I thought she was bright. She certainly knew most everything that Carrie's daughter knew and Zoë was already three.

The TV was on in the living room and some cop show was playing. As it was, whenever Jessie saw a man in uniform, she automatically thought of Jason. "When's Daddy coming home?" she asked suddenly in her sweet, little voice. "I want Daddy."

So do I, I thought achingly, but I said, "Daddy will be home as soon as he can, sweetie. He wants to be here with us, but the Army needs him right now."

She puffed out her tiny chest and defiantly folded her arms in front of it, pouting and knitting her little brow into a stern, dark line. "No, Mommy, we need him."

I couldn't argue with her logic so I didn't say anything. I turned to a different channel and pulled her basket of books out from under the coffee table. Before long, she forgot all about the policeman and her daddy. But I didn't. The truth is, Jessie was used to Jason being away. He'd been gone more often than he was home for as long as she'd been alive. She didn't know anything was out of the ordinary about the way she was being brought up, but I was definitely getting tired of the situation. Already, Jason had missed so many of her childhood discoveries and he was bound to miss even more. I began to wonder if I would have to face every aspect of our children's lives alone.

Will Jason see Amber's first steps? Jessie's first day of kindergarten? Her graduation? Amber's wedding?

I knew I was getting way ahead of myself, but I couldn't help it. The more I thought about raising my daughters on my own, the angrier I got. I ardently believed that Jason should be with us—that home was where he belonged. I agreed with him in the beginning that a military career was the right choice for him, but that was before we had children. Now I was having second thoughts.

What if something happens to him? I thought with growing dismay. I can't raise two little girls on my own!

Jessie and I fell asleep on the couch. It was after midnight when I woke up with her sleeping on my arm. I slid out from under her and shook away the pins and needles. I carried her upstairs to her bed and then lay down myself. I stared at the ceiling for what seemed like hours before I finally fell asleep.

The next morning I was over my anger and back to worrying about my husband's safety.

How did mothers and wives do it all these years? I asked myself over and over again. And nowadays, even husbands are the ones at home worrying. I don't know if I'll ever get used to it.

At ten-fifteen I put Amber in her stroller, instructed Jessie to grab hold, and we headed across the courtyard to the mailboxes. I told myself not to get my hopes up. I figured if I didn't expect anything, I couldn't be disappointed.

Jessie talked about the clouds drifting overhead and her favorite cartoon and I tried to pay attention like a good mommy. The mailbox was empty. I slammed the door shut and turned my key to lock it with an angry twist. Suddenly, I was mad all over again—at Jason, the Army, and the United States Postal Service.

I was so tired of living alone; I wanted my husband back. I was tired of being both father and mother to my babies. I was tired of handling every little crisis on my own. I was tired of being brave. I wanted someone else to do it all for a while.

Why doesn't Jason write—or, better yet—call?

I wanted to hear his voice.

As it was, it'd been almost two weeks since I heard about the ambushed engineering battalion.

If something happened to Jason, surely I would've been notified by now. Unless they aren't releasing the names of the dead or injured until they can all be identified. Or maybe there's some kind of ongoing investigation into the incident and the media isn't at liberty to release information at this time.

Back in the apartment I spent the day writing a six-page letter to my husband, pouring out my loneliness and frustration through every word. I knew it wasn't at all fair to him since he was so far away and couldn't possibly help with my problems at home, but I unloaded on him nevertheless. I told him about how upset Jessie was because he wasn't home with us. I told him that his place was here in our home with Jessie and Amber and me, protecting his family. I told him I wasn't any good at being a soldier's wife; I told him that I wanted a husband with a regular job. I told him that he'd received good training during his stint and surely, he wouldn't have to go back to the candle factory after his term was up, but—

I was finished with being a soldier's wife.

Before I could lose my nerve I stamped the letter and dropped it into the mailbox on the corner.

There, I thought. If that letter ever reaches him, he'll know exactly how his wife and children feel.

My life became a dreary, nonstop cycle of going to school, feeding the girls and putting them to bed, and then sitting up late at night on the Internet. Lord knows, there were plenty of chat rooms where I could vent my anger.

Then my psych professor asked me to speak with him after class one day. Even before I approached his desk, I knew exactly what he was going to say.

"Robin, your performance on your last paper was not up to your potential." He gave me a grave look. "You know, it isn't only your time you're wasting when you don't apply yourself in my class."

I felt like a kindergartner being reprimanded by the principal. "I know, Dr. Van Housen. I'm sorry."

His stern demeanor relaxed a little. "I know you have a lot on your mind with your husband's deployment. Have you heard from him recently?"

Tears sprang to my eyes and I looked away, embarrassed. I did not want to start crying in front of him. "Not in four weeks."

"I'm sorry." He shuffled the papers on his desk and tried to look stern again. "But the best thing for you to do is stay busy. Here." He handed me a piece of paper. "Turn in this assignment by next week. It may help bring up your dismal average."

46

I knew for a fact that my grade point average wasn't that dismal. He was trying to help me deal with Jason's absence in his own way. "Thank you, Dr. Van Housen." I tucked the paper into my tote bag and turned to leave.

"Mrs. Hennessey?"

I turned to look at him.

"There are support groups and counselors available on the base if you need to talk to someone. You're not completely alone in this."

"Yes, sir." I gave him a weak smile and left the lecture hall.

Back at home, after I paid the babysitter I took the girls over to Carrie's. "My psych professor told me about some support groups here on base for those of us who have spouses overseas," I told her.

She nodded. "I used to go to the meetings, but I usually came home missing Derek more than ever."

"What if we go together?"

She shrugged. "We could try it. They have facilities for the kids, too, you know. I guess it'd be nice to get out of the apartment for a change and talk to someone who understands what it's like playing Mommy and Daddy at the same time for months on end."

I burst into tears. "Oh, Carrie! I thought I was the only one who felt like that!"

She smiled and hugged me. "No way, honey—we all feel that way and we're all going through the exact same thing right now. It's not fun, but you get used to it after awhile."

I drew away and sank down into a kitchen chair. "I don't know if I want to get used to it."

"Yes, you do. After all, you love Jason, right? And just think of all the good things the military offers that you can't find in any other workplace."

All of a sudden I remembered the pamphlets Jason brought home when we were first married. It all looked and sounded so exciting back then. I supposed it was still exciting. They just didn't feature photos of lonely spouses on those pamphlets—and for good reasons, too, I realized.

Three nights later Carrie and I and our three girls all showed up at our first support group meeting. There were about twenty people already there and in one corner of the room there was a bunch of toys. Older kids played in groups with a smaller area cordoned off for the preschoolers. Jessie and Zoë held hands and hesitantly joined a group; I pushed Amber's stroller over to a half-circle of folding chairs and Carrie and I sat down.

Within minutes we were part of the group. I hadn't realized that so many military spouses have the same fears and concerns that I do. When it was my turn to introduce myself to the group I told them that

47

I hadn't heard from my husband in five weeks. Everyone nodded in sympathetic, been-there/done-that understanding; no one acted like my situation was unique. Strange as it may seem, that made me feel a whole lot better.

By the time we left an hour later, Carrie and I had decided we'd be back for the next meeting on Friday. "That wasn't so bad, huh?" Carrie remarked. "If anything, I actually feel closer to Derek this time. Now I can imagine him sharing his concerns about Zoë and me with his friends over there."

I nodded, smiling for the first time in what seemed like years. "That's how I feel. But at least Jason knows where we are."

"I guess so. But all in all, I think the soldiers have it a lot worse than we do, you know? I mean, yes—they know where their families are, for the most part. But they also know that they're missing out on so much of their kids' lives. Just look at my situation—Derek's missed out on Zoë's first steps and her first tooth, and he wasn't here when his mom had her heart attack. I mean, do you ever stop to think about how helpless they must feel, knowing full well that we need them and desperately want them here—and that they can't do a darn thing about it?"

I thought of the nasty letter I mailed to Jason. All at once I felt sick to my stomach, realizing that I never should've written to him while I was upset.

I shook my head miserably in shame, feeling my shoulders sag. "But I'm so terrible at this, Carrie—I'm terrible at all of it. I hate being the only one responsible for Jessie and Amber. As it is, these days, I don't even feel like I can take care of myself, so how can I possibly be expected to protect them and do all the things that both a good mother and a good father should? I tell you, Carrie—I'm useless without Jason."

She patted my hand. "That's not true, Robin. You're a good mother—a great mother, even. I know you miss Jason terribly, but you can take care of those girls without him; after all, you've been doing it for as long as they've been alive, haven't you? And you're doing a terrific job."

How I wanted to believe her.

After dinner on Wednesday I sat down at the table and focused on finishing my paper for my psych class as it was due the next day and I knew I hadn't spent enough time on it. Dr. Van Housen was throwing me a bone, offering me the opportunity to earn extra credit toward my final grade in his class, and I didn't want to disappoint him again. Two hours later I was just finishing up when the phone rang. I figured it was probably Carrie calling to remind me that our support group was scheduled to meet the next night. At our last meeting someone had suggested planning a chili cook-off and we both wanted to participate.

"Hello?"

Silence on the other end of the line.

"Hello?" I said again, louder. I wasn't in the mood to deal with a prank call or a telemarketer.

I heard a few clicks and a whole lot of static . . . and then my husband's voice. "Robin? Honey, is that you?"

I burst into tears. "Jason? Oh, I can't believe it! Oh, where have you been?"

He laughed. "Sweetheart, you know where I've been."

I laughed, too, even though I was still crying. "Oh, I know, I know! I'm just being silly, I guess! Oh, but, Jason—I've been so worried!"

"Yeah, I kinda figured as much. I got a really nasty letter the other day."

I tightened my grip on the phone and wished I were holding him, instead. "Oh, Jason, I am so, so sorry about that. I was really upset the day I wrote it."

He chuckled. "I could tell." He chuckled again and it sounded like music to my ears.

Jessie jumped up from where she'd been playing on the floor in front of me. "Daddy! Daddy! I wanna talk to Daddy!" she cried excitedly.

Even nine-month-old Amber acted like she knew who was on the line. We were only able to talk for about five minutes, but we tried to squeeze six months' worth of "I love yous" and "I miss yous" into that small amount of time.

At the end of the call, I apologized again for my letter. "I was angry with you for leaving me here to take care of every little thing," I explained, "but I guess I'll just have to learn to handle it from now on."

"Sweetheart, you're not really finished with being a soldier's wife, are you?"

I chuckled and wiped my tears away. "I guess not. After all—I don't know how to be any other kind!"

"Good. Because you're stuck with me, baby. You know that, don't you?"

"And you're stuck with me. And I wouldn't want it any other way, Jason."

"Listen, baby—I gotta go. But I love you and I'll be thinking of you and our girls every second of the days and nights to come until I'm back at home with all my girls, right where I belong."

"I love you, too, sweetheart."

"I've written you several letters, by the way; they should get to you soon. Kiss the girls for me, baby. I miss you and I love you with all my heart."

"I miss you and love you, too. Stay safe, baby."

I managed to pass my psychology course and I did well in my other classes. When it was time to register for the next semester I decided to major in English. I'd decided that I wanted to teach high school English someday and I figured that even if we ever got stationed in Japan, there'd still be schools that would need English teachers. As it was, it would take me at least three more years to earn my degree since I couldn't study full time. I already have a full-time job being Jessie and Amber's mommy.

Then I got a phone call one evening and two days later, the girls and I were waiting on the dock when the ship carrying my husband came in.

Jason's been stateside for six months now. I've always suspected that I can conceive easily and, indeed—guess what? We're expecting another baby!

Today, I remember the promise I made to myself before I married Jason—the promise that said I would never settle for what life threw at me simply because it was easier than fighting for what I want. Today, I am no longer that woman who cried at the mere thought of being alone; I have learned to trust in myself and to take care of my girls, and my husband—and to take care of me. It will never be easy, being both Mom and Dad to our girls, but there will be times when I have no choice. The thing that helps me stay strong through it all, no matter what life and war bring our way, is the important lesson I learned the hard way—

A soldier's wife can handle anything.
THE END

LOVE'S STRONG TIES

Silver wings shining in the sunlight. The words of an old country song played in my mind as I stood at the window of the airport and watched my tall, handsome husband, Mike, board the plane that would send him on his way to Iraq. I bit my lip hard to keep from crying as he turned to wave at me. I would not let him see me cry; the tears would come later. Tonight, as I lie alone in our king-sized bed, the tears would flow.

Silver wings slowly fading out of sight. I watched until the plane was a mere speck in the sky before turning to leave. Then, still biting my lip, I rushed outside to my car and lay my head on the steering wheel. The tears would not wait until tonight.

I drove home in a daze. I dreaded walking in that door and facing Mike's dad. His dad had been living with us for six years now, ever since Mike's mom had died of breast cancer. I had come to love Daddy Jack as if he were my own father. I really did not know my father, who had divorced my mother when I was four and married his secretary—the age-old story. Through the years I had gotten cards and gifts, and occasionally, when he was in Chicago, he would take me out to dinner. Since my marriage to Mike ten years ago, our communication had dwindled down to an exchange of birthday cards. Meanwhile, Mom had married again and moved on with her life. She and Bob, her husband, now lived in Florida, and Mike and I had spent a week with them before he was called up by the National Guard.

As I pulled up in the driveway, I could see Daddy Jack out in the back raking leaves. Almost all the leaves had fallen now; only a few clung to the old oak tree up front, as if reluctant to give way to the coming winter. I shivered as I got out of the car and pulled my sweater about me. I also had to face the coming winter.

"Where is Mike?" Daddy Jack was striding toward the car. Oh God, not now. Don't let him have one of his spells now. I can't take it right now. Something was happening to Daddy Jack. Every so often he would suffer spells of forgetfulness, even once losing his way when he went for a walk. The following day, he would be fine, and Mike and I decided it was just old age.

Remember when you lost the car at the mall and it was right in front of you? Mike had laughed. But slowly, for the past year, Daddy Jack was getting more and more forgetful, and worse, he was having nightmares about his days as a helicopter pilot in Vietnam. Since Mike had been called up, it seemed that my father-in-law's mind was wandering more and more. I felt it had something to do with the war in Iraq and his son being called to duty. His old memories of the war in Vietnam were getting all mixed up with the war in Iraq.

"Daddy Jack," I said as he approached, "Mike had to leave, don't you remember? He's on his way to Iraq. I just took him to the airport."

"Oh, yes," he gave an embarrassed laugh. "Now I remember. For a moment, I thought he was with you."

"It's okay, let's go in and make dinner. How about some spaghetti? I'd love that for dinner." Spaghetti was his pride and joy, and Mike always made a big deal about his dad's cooking skills. I knew I would be lucky to force down a forkful, but I needed to bring some degree of normalcy back to the household.

After dinner I lay in bed, my face turned to the open window where a full moon bathed the room in golden light. Just last night I had lain here in Mike's arms, and we had made love for the last time. For the hundredth time, I wished we could have made a baby, but that dream had gone by the wayside. After years of infertility, we had been looking into adoption when Mike was called up. Now that was also on the back burner.

I couldn't sleep. My mind kept going back to when I had first met Mike, and our years together. It was hard to believe ten years had gone by. I had just finished a two-year nursing course and had gotten a job in Dr. Frank's office. Mom and her new husband had sold their house in Chicago and moved into a condo in Florida. This led to my getting my first apartment and starting to live on my own.

Dr. Frank was a friend of Mom's. She had been a registered nurse in the hospital where he was an obstetrician, and she paved the way for me to get the job, which I loved dearly. It was a happy environment, and I dreamed of the day I would marry and have my own children. Meanwhile, I reveled in the joy of the young—and the not-so-young—mothers who came in for prenatal visits. It was fun to help with the sonograms and to see a couple exchange tender glances when the sex of the child showed up on film. Amongst all the mothers, a favorite of the staff was Mirabella, a young Mexican American whose husband, Jose, had just been killed in a holdup at the convenience store where he had worked. After four daughters, she had found out this one was a boy. We all felt we had a stake in this pregnancy. The baby's name was to be Jose Jr.

One morning, shortly after I had begun work, Mirabella showed up at the office complaining of pain and bleeding. Dr. Frank did a quick check and yelled, "Call 911." I was holding Mirabella's hand when the paramedic rushed in, and I looked up into the bluest eyes I had ever seen. And that is how I met Mike.

Mirabella recovered, Baby Jose spent months in premature care, and I married Mike six months later. We made a solemn vow to name our first daughter Mirabella. We planned to have several kids since neither of us had any brothers or sisters.

The first two years went according to our plan. We would both work, save our money, and buy a house. Then would come the children. The house part came true; we found a lovely older home for a decent price and spent weekends fixing it up. Every Saturday found us painting or sanding floors, and each Saturday night found us on our oversized sofa with a huge pizza between us and the latest video release showing on the TV screen. It was a time of happiness, a time to look ahead, a time to dream.

But dreams have a way of vanishing into thin air, and the first cloud on our happiness came when Mike's mom called with the news that she had breast cancer. She was upbeat at first, but a month of chemotherapy drained her resolve and did little to cure her. In six months she was dead, and Daddy Jack was left to wander about their big house alone. It was sad to see him, a military man and disciplined to the core, fall apart. Mike insisted he sell the house and get a condo. "You can travel, Dad, see the world," he told him.

"My world is gone," said his father.

"He has to come live with us," I told Mike. "He needs his family, and he can help us when we start having children. Just think, Mike, a granddad in the house! And it will be good for your father."

Mike kissed me. "Thanks, honey, I had been thinking about that but I didn't want to push you. I wasn't sure how you would feel about an in-law living with us."

But the children didn't come. A year went by and we finally sought infertility help. Nothing worked. The doctors could not find anything serious, just a minor anatomical problem with my fallopian tubes for which I underwent a minor procedure. Still, nothing. By then it had been five years, Daddy Jack was a beloved fixture in our lives, and we started talking adoption. My work at the clinic still filled a void in my life, and Mike stayed happily employed with Memorial Hospital. In helping others, we helped ourselves.

All these years Mike had been going away one weekend a month for National Guard training. We never dreamed he would ever be called up for anything but a national disaster.

Then came 9/11, and we watched in horror as the Twin Towers fell and people died. The sunny days of fixing up the house and having backyard barbecues were now a distant part of the past. America had changed, and so had we. As a National Guardsman, Mike knew there was danger ahead. "We have to fight back," he said, "we have to defend our country."

When the war turned toward Iraq and the TV blared the invasion of Baghdad over the airways, Mike started to prepare us for the possibility that he would be called.

53

"Oh, no," I told him, "it will all be over soon."

But the war dragged on. They found Saddam and still it went on. There were more casualties; the head nurse at the clinic lost her son. The war was hitting home.

And then in May, when the world was welcoming spring and the smell of flowers filled the air, Mike came home and took me in his arms.

"They called up our unit today, Melinda. It's just a matter of time until we're sent to Iraq." He stroked my hair. "It's not just us, baby, they're calling up reserves all over."

I forced myself to be brave, but inside I wanted to scream. Mike was the rock I leaned on. Mike made everything better when everything went wrong. But as he hugged me I felt the tension in him, and I knew it was my time to step up to the plate.

"Well, you won't have to worry about me and your dad, we'll have each other. That old army guy will keep me on the straight and narrow." I smiled through tears. "Maybe it will all get better over there before you go."

Mike shook his head, his blue eyes holding a hint of tears. "No, honey, I think it's going to get worse before it gets better, and the U.S. Army is in a fight for its life. But my dad fought a war worse than this, and now it's my turn."

Despite my brave comments about Daddy Jack, my heart was sinking. I was noticing things Mike had not. Daddy Jack didn't only lose things—he put them in bizarre places. I had found his glasses in the fridge and his wallet in a birdhouse. When we were talking, he often stopped mid-sentence, and he never remembered what we'd had for dinner the night before. He had known our neighbor, Sandy, for six years, but he would ask me what her name was almost every day when he saw her in the yard. Separately, these incidents would not be a cause for alarm; collectively, however, it was clear that something was wrong.

I had brought the incidents to Mike's attention only a few times, and now I did not dare. If nothing else, I would keep his father's problem from him, let him remember the strength and courage of his military dad.

And now, Mike was gone, flying into the unknown—silver wings taking him away. I was alone with a sweet but disturbed old man and a desperate yearning to have had a child.

The days passed. I went to work each morning, looking wistfully at shiny-eyed pregnant women. It made me wish, now more than ever, that I had a child. If something happens to Mike, if he doesn't come back, if only we had adopted , if only, if only. . .

The month of November was cold. On Thanksgiving it snowed.

I bought a turkey and all the trimmings, keeping Daddy Jack busy and close to my side. He was in good spirits, even telling me about when Mike was a tiny tot and he cried when he saw the poor turkey on the table.

"Mike has a soft heart," he told me, and with tears in my eyes, I agreed.

That night after dinner, after putting things away, I lay on the sofa, gazing into the fire. Suddenly, I heard a crash in the kitchen. Daddy Jack had gone to bed and I could not imagine what had happened. I rushed in and there was Daddy Jack. He had dropped the platter where the turkey had rested and was holding the turkey high above his head, ready to fling it into the trash.

"Daddy Jack," I yelled." What are you doing?"

"I should have disposed of this earlier," he said, his eyes vacantly staring over my head. "The boy hated it, oh how he cried. My Mike cried and I made him eat it."

"Mike likes turkey now, Daddy Jack." I approached him and took it from his hand. "Mike loves you very much. He told me." I kept repeating that Mike loved him until I had him lying quietly in bed.

After cleaning up the mess, I made hot tea and sat at the kitchen table. Daddy Jack is getting worse. He might hurt himself or me. What am I going to tell Mike? I won't say anything yet. If it's Alzheimer's, it will be slow, gradual. I'll just take precautions—no knives or scissors. But what about while I'm at work? My mind raced on. I'll ask Sandy first thing tomorrow, I'll ask her to watch him closely. Sandy lived alone and didn't work. She spent a lot of time puttering about her big old house and working in her yard.

I couldn't sleep that night. I had not been feeling well for weeks now. I found it hard to get up in the morning and felt sluggish all day. I wondered if I was anemic. Tomorrow I would double up on the vitamins and maybe add some iron to my diet. It could also be the approaching holidays and the stress at home. When I talked to Mike, who was now in Baghdad, I was careful to sound upbeat, but I really felt terribly alone.

As Christmas approached, I could no longer blame stress on my physical well-being. I felt lousy. Daddy Jack had not gotten any worse, and he had only long intervals of being forgetful. Sandy watched him carefully, often inviting him home with her or coming over to watch TV with him. Mike was working in a field hospital and not subject to the continuous explosives that were blowing up so many of our troops. All in all, I should've been feeling relief. I didn't. I felt horrible.

Dr. Frank noticed. One day he called me into his office and confronted me. "Melinda, I want to run some tests on you. You've lost weight; you drag around like an old lady. Let's check you out."

"Dr. Frank, it's just Mike being away and his dad's condition—" I started to say.

"Could you be pregnant?" He smiled.

"You know we can't have children, Dr. Frank." Tears filled my eyes. How cruel of him to say that when he knows I'd give anything to be pregnant.

They did the blood work. I was anemic, but not only anemic, I was almost two months pregnant. After years of futile hope, Mike and I were going to have a baby.

That night, I emailed Mike. "Hello, Daddy, dreams do come true." The next day, Mike called, his voice filled with tears.

"Have you told Dad? What did he say?" he asked. "Please take a picture of yourself." His words stumbled over each other, and when we hung up, we were both in tears.

Christmas was joyous. I told Daddy Jack about the baby, and he went around with a smile on his face. There were a few days when he would forget and ask me where the baby was, but those times did not worry me as they once would have. Sandy was a fixture in our house now. She had no family and was fast becoming like a mother to me. We put up a tree, played Christmas carols, and made a video for Mike. It snowed on Christmas Day, and we even made a snowman. In the video, Daddy Jack is laughing, poised with a snowball in his hand, aiming it at Sandy. It was a day to make memories.

The days flew by. My morning sickness subsided and I was no longer anemic. Only one cloud marred my happiness—with the exception of Mike's absence—Daddy Jack was growing worse. It was April now, and we could not keep him in the house as we had in the winter. He was growing more imitable, and he often accused Sandy of stealing his garden tools. Sandy was a godsend: she never grew angry or frustrated, she just calmly reassured him when he said abusive things to her. With me, he was relatively calm, but there were times when he insisted that Mike was not in the Army. He was also growing more careless about his appearance, and this hurt me most of all. This once-proud, old soldier who never came down in the morning without his crisp khakis and starched shirt, walked around with his shirt buttoned crookedly and his pants unzipped. It broke my heart.

And I could not confide in Mike. If only I can hold on until Mike comes home, until the baby is born; then we can decide what to do.

One bright spring morning I took Daddy Jack to a doctor that Dr. Frank had referred me to, a specialist in Alzheimer's and Dementia. My father-in-law was coherent and cooperative on this day, looking out the window at the passing landscape and commenting on the flowering trees.

56

"Gertrude loved the springtime," he said. "When we were stationed in Georgia, there was a dogwood tree in our yard. She could not wait for it to bloom every Easter." He turned to me with tears in his eyes. "I sure do miss Gertrude."

As we sat in the waiting room, it was clear that this was a roomful of people waiting for the nail in their coffin. Next to me sat a woman about my age, holding the hand of a grey haired well-groomed woman of about sixty. The woman's clothes spoke of class, as did her low cultured voice. But the eyes, large and dark, were vacant. She turned to me and in a very conversational voice, said clearly, "We are here to get the baby. We have adopted a darling little girl."

The young woman shook her head at me. "I am that little girl," she said ruefully.

"She's too old to adopt," Daddy Jack chimed in, then looking about him with suspicion, he noticed the other men and women and sensed immediately that something was wrong.

"Take me home, Melinda. I'm not crazy, I'm just forgetful. Just wait until I tell Mike about the stunt you're pulling." He was agitated, heading for the door. A nurse restrained him, and soon we were seated in an examining room where Dr. Jonas, a kindly, white-haired man, administered a light sedative and told me to wait outside. "He's a little miffed at you right now." He smiled. "This always happens with the care giver."

Up until now, I had not thought of that word. Now, it hit me. Daddy Jack does have that dreaded disease. Oh, Mike, what am I going to do?

A few days later, after all tests were in, Dr. Jonas called and confirmed that Daddy Jack had Alzheimer's. He wasn't ready yet for long-term care, but there was a medicine he wanted to try. He would need to be watched carefully.

I spoke to Sandy, and she agreed to live with us until the baby came and Mike and I could make a decision about Daddy Jack's future care. She would tend to her own duties and chores while I was home, but spend every night with us until the baby came.

With Sandy in the guest bedroom next to Daddy Jack, I could sleep peacefully. The medicine was helping him; he was less agitated and still recognized both Sandy and me. Now I could focus on the baby, feel him inside me, a part of me, a part of my husband. Yes, I knew it was a he. I'd had the sonogram a month before and had told Mike that night on the phone.

I had big dreams for this baby. I was already buying a wardrobe—tiny shirts, soft as down pajamas, tiny sneakers that would not be worn for months. Mom was ecstatic. She came for a week, bringing a suitcase full of wrapped gifts from her Florida friends, and she took me out for a new hairdo and new maternity outfits. I shared everything with Mike in long letters, emails, and pictures.

Then, one day in June, it happened—Daddy Jack got much worse. It had been raining all day, and dark clouds hovered over the city. Dr. Frank was late to the clinic, having had two deliveries the night before, and we all worked late seeing patients who had been waiting for hours. It was dark, and I was on the freeway coming home when my cell phone rang. It was Sandy, her voice frantic.

"Melinda, Jack is nowhere to be found. He was napping, and when I went to call him down for tea, his bed was empty. Oh goodness, I shouldn't be worrying you, but it's raining and—"

"Call the police, Sandy," I said. "Check the garden, he was talking about planting some vegetables or something this morning, but first, call the police."

A squad car was waiting in front of the house when I got home. A young officer was inside taking down information, asking for a photograph, learning about the Alzheimer's. He looked up as I came in, noticing my pregnant state and assuring me that we would find my father-in-law.

The night wore on and there was no news. Then, at four in the morning, the doorbell rang. The young officer led a bedraggled and very wet Daddy Jack by the hand. "I believe this belongs to you," he smiled.

"Those rice paddies are hell, Gertrude. It rains all the time in Vietnam," Daddy Jack told me.

I knew something had to be done. Only six weeks were left before the baby came, and I could not hold on any longer, even with the help of Sandy. I needed to call Dr. Jonas and ask where I could get help for my poor, sweet father-in-law. The time had come.

We took Daddy Jack to an assisted living home where he would be watched carefully all the time. I held back tears as we got ready to leave, even though I liked the staff already, especially a young nurse named Ellen.

"Gertrude, now you hurry back," Daddy Jack said anxiously. "If you wait until I get these seeds planted, I'll go with you." He started fumbling in the drawer of the bedside table. "Now where are the seeds?"

Ellen motioned for us to leave and slipped out the door behind us. "He'll be alright," she whispered. "It's sad, but he really doesn't know what's going on. I'll fix his lunch and he'll settle down. Somehow, it seems like food soothes them. What is his favorite food?"

"Spaghetti," I whispered, the tears welling up. "And use extra oregano."

In the car, I broke down. Sandy held me close. "I have a

surprise," she said. "Your mom is coming in tonight. She is going to stay until the baby comes."

With Mom came comfort and support. She had raised me alone, had withstood divorce and heartache, and come out on top. She settled in, and soon she and Sandy had the house running like clockwork. I would be quitting work in June, and they planned to pamper me right up till the baby's birth. Except for the nagging worry about Mike, my life was happy.

But the war was getting worse. More and more soldiers were being killed by roadside bombs. Things were not going as we had believed. I watched the evening news night after night, and I began to worry. Mike was vague about what he was doing now. In phone calls, he would sometimes let it slip that he was in dangerous territory.

"The road to the Baghdad airport is called 'the road of death,'" he said one night.

"Have you been on it?" I asked anxiously.

"Oh, a while back. Don't worry, I'm a paramedic, remember? We don't go on patrol."

He didn't have to tell me. I knew that every time a tank rolled, it was likely that someone would be killed or wounded.

One night as I sat before the TV, Mom came in, took the remote from my hand, and inserted a movie into the DVD player.

"You are not going to watch any more of this tonight," she said firmly. So we watched a comedy, and I tried to enjoy the loaded sundae she placed in my hand.

"What would I do without you?" I asked her.

She smiled and kissed me softly. "We've been through a lot together," she said.

Sandy, Mom, and I visited Daddy Jack almost every day, taking him his favorite food or a magazine with pictures of gardens or travelogues of some of the places he had been while in the military. Sometimes he knew me, other times he didn't. Often he called me Gertrude.

One day, he looked at a postcard picture of a cathedral in Rome for a long time.

"Gertrude, I want you to go to this church," he said firmly, handing me the picture. "I've been there. I took Mike. I want you to see it."

"That church has an exact replica here in Chicago," Mom told me on the way home.

"Mike was never in Rome, Mom. Do you think Daddy Jack took him to the church here in Chicago?"

"I don't know, but if I were you, I would go see for myself."

I taped the picture to my bathroom mirror. It had a certain mystique about it; it appealed to me.

Two weeks before my due date, the office staff gave me a shower. It was given at the home of one of the nurses, and she had gone all out in decorating the house. The theme was bluebirds, for the bluebird of happiness, and there was even cookies in the shape of bluebirds. I felt like a queen, especially when Dr. Frank dropped by with a brand new soccer ball for the baby. Laughing, he bent over to kiss me.

"Now, don't get too excited and have that boy tonight," he laughed. "I have a baseball game to watch."

Then, a nurse called for quiet. Going to the TV, she inserted a video. There was Mike, a big grin on his face, surrounded by several of his buddies.

He lifted a glass, surely it was water, and toasted me. "Here's to my beautiful wife and our beautiful baby. See you soon, honey." The guys all cheered, and so did everyone in the room. Surrounded by gifts and friends, I could not have been happier at that moment.

For the next two weeks, what should have been a time of "nesting" became the worst two weeks of my life. I did not hear from Mike. All communication ceased. Suicide bombers were in the news every day, as well as roadside bombings of Humvees. I found myself glued to CNN, expecting to hear that someone from Mike's unit had been blown up. By now, I was convinced something had happened, that he was dead, that God had given me this child because He planned to take Mike home to heaven. My imagination went wild, and no one could calm me.

In July, I forced myself to go and visit Daddy Jack. I had not been in a while. He was strangely calm, and still convinced that I was Gertrude. Smiling, he touched my stomach and pronounced, "We are going to have a boy, Gertrude." Then he grew agitated and started rummaging through his dresser drawer.

"Daddy Jack, what are you looking for?" I asked.

"The picture, Gertrude, of the church. I want you to go to the church where I took Mike."

Soothingly, I replied, "I'll go, Daddy Jack. I promise."

On the way home I called Mom. "Can you please get me the address of that church, the one in my bathroom mirror, and call me back?"

I followed Mom's directions, and sure enough, there it was in downtown Chicago, a stately stone church that must have been there for a hundred years. I parked in the back and tried a side door. It was unlocked. Cautiously, I entered and sat in a front pew. I had only been inside a Catholic church once or twice, but this was exotic. Statues of saints lined the walls, and Mary and Joseph looked down on me from stained glass windows. I did not know why Daddy Jack had sent me here, or even if he knew himself what he was saying, but a strange calm fell over me and I knelt and prayed. God, please let Mike be safe. Please let him see his son. Then I added those age-old words, Not my will but thine be done.

That night I went into labor, and Mom and Sandy took me to the hospital. It was twelve o'clock on July fourth, and Dr. Frank teased me as he examined me, "Leave it to our Melinda to bring forth a baby amidst the explosion of fireworks."

However, the birth did not proceed as intended, and at three in the morning, Dr. Frank informed me he would be doing a Caesarean section.

Sometime that day, I awoke to the sound of the nurse's voice in my ear. "Come on, wake up, Melinda, you have a brand new boy and a brand new visitor." Struggling through the haze of sleep, I thought I saw Mike's face above me. There were tears on his cheeks. Why is Mike here and why is he crying? Then it all became clear. I was in the hospital, I'd had my baby, and it was Mike standing by my bed. With a cry of joy, I reached for him and was soon enveloped in his arms.

"Oh, Mike, how? When? I thought you were dead," I sobbed.

"I couldn't miss my son's birth, now could I? After ten years, I'm a dad. Don't worry, I'll explain later. Now they're going to bring in our son."

The baby was beautiful, with lots of dark hair and Mike's blue eyes. I kept looking from his face to Mike's. I could not believe Mike was here beside me and that we had a son, a son we had already named for Mike's father, to be known hereafter as little Jack.

To my sorrow, I learned that Mike was only home for two weeks. He had been in a battle in Fallujah two weeks earlier and had flown into Germany with several wounded soldiers. Somehow, he had wrangled a quick leave because of the impending birth and the illness of his father.

A few days later, we went to see Daddy Jack and took the baby with us. Mike's father did not recognize him, and he thought the baby was Mike. He kept saying over and over, "We have a boy, Gertrude. What a good-looking boy."

However, as we left and Mike bent over to kiss his dad, Daddy Jack put his hand on Mike's face and said, "My soldier boy." Those words seemed to lighten Mike's mood, and as we walked toward the car, he said softly, "My dad was quite a guy."

As we drove through the city, I had an inspiration. "Mike, let's go by a church. I want to tell you something." I wanted to see if Mike remembered being there with his dad.

We entered and knelt in the font pew. Mike kept looking at me quizzically. Seconds later, he grasped my arm. "I've been here before," he said. "I can't remember when, but I've been here."

We left the church, the scent of burning candles and incense trailing with us. We were quiet in the car for a few minutes before I spoke.

"Mike, your dad kept telling me to go there, that he had been there with you. What do you remember?"

"I was small, I remember, and Mom was very sick—in the hospital. Dad was kneeling. He told me to ask God to make Mom well. That must have been when she had the first bout with breast cancer. It didn't come back again for almost twenty years, Melinda. You know, I never connected it with that visit to the church."

So that's why he told me to go to the church. He knew somehow that Mike was in danger. Thank God I went there.

A year has passed since that day. Mike had another tour of duty and will be coming home in a few weeks. Another miracle occurred, and I am pregnant again, this time with a girl—Mirabella. We lost Daddy Jack not long after little Jack was born. In a way, of course, we lost him earlier than that. With his terrible disease, the soul leaves, and we are left with only the body to care for. I think Daddy Jack's soul did a lot of watching out for Mike and me long before his body died.

This much I know: My little family will visit that church often in the future, and we will always light a candle for the miracles in our lives.

THE END

DANGEROUSLY IN LOVE
Does love really conquer all?

The noise was deafening as we waited for the plane to land, bringing our loved ones back from Iraq. Babies, most of whom had never seen their fathers, cried. Children, like my two boys, grew impatient and became rowdy. I heard the same question from them a hundred times. "When is Daddy going to be here?"

It was a year ago when we gathered to see the troops off. Now, in a matter of minutes, my husband, Darren, would be back with his family. I anxiously awaited his arms around me, and the touch of his kiss. He would smile his lazy smile; tease the boys about how much they'd grown, or how long their hair was. And then, we would go home.

Every night, before drifting off to sleep, I would think about Darren's return. Though I carried fear in my heart, terrified that he might be hurt or worse yet—killed—I fought the fear by praying and hoping. Now, he was coming home to us, safe and in one piece. It was time to rejoice.

An hour and ten minutes later, the plane finally landed. Mayhem erupted as the men walked off the plane. We were held back until they were dismissed.

An hour and ten minutes later, the plane finally landed. Mayhem erupted as the men walked off the plane. We were held back until they were dismissed.

Afterward, people began to run to their soldier. It was Connor, our oldest son, who spotted Darren first.

"Mom, there he is!" Connor shouted. "There's Dad!"

Connor, and his brother, Jeremy, broke from me and ran to their father. Darren saw them and hurried toward them. He hugged each boy, and then lifted Jeremy into his arms. With Connor keeping stride with his dad, they made their way to me.

"I've missed you, Cassie," Darren said, looking deeply into my eyes. He put Jeremy down, took me in his arms and kissed me—just the way I'd imagined it every night he'd been away.

Tears ran down my cheeks. It was the happiest moment of my life. The man I'd loved since I was a teenager was back in my arms. "Can we go home now?" I asked.

Darren nodded. "Let me get my gear."

That night was a celebration. I cooked all of Darren's favorite foods. Family and neighbors came by to say hello, but thankfully, they didn't stay long. Selfish as it may sound, I wanted my husband to myself.

After everyone left and the boys were tucked into bed, I hurried to our room to shower and change. I'd bought an especially sexy teddy that I hoped Darren would like.

He did, though it didn't stay on me very long.

When Darren and I made love, it seemed as though we'd never been apart. As though Iraq had never existed, that the National Guard hadn't taken my Darren away from me for a year. I fell asleep in his arms, happy and content.

The next morning when I awakened, he wasn't in bed. I glanced at the clock. It was barely 6:00 a.m. I put on my robe and began searching for Darren. I found him sitting in on the deck, staring up at the sky.

"Good morning, darling," I said. "Why didn't you wake me? We could have coffee together out here."

"I don't want any coffee," he said in a flat, uninvolved tone, while never taking his eyes off the sky.

I struggled for something to say. Should I ask him about Iraq? I wondered. The cold, indifferent way that he sat, stopped me. He might not be ready to talk about Iraq, yet.

"Guess I'll get dressed," I said, and I went back to the bedroom. I hoped that when I saw Darren again, he would be in a better mood.

I went outside to the deck. He was still sitting there, exactly the way I'd left him. "Ready for coffee, now?" I asked.

"Cassie, when I want a cup of coffee, I'll make it. Stop nagging me," he snapped. "I just want some time to myself. Is that too much to ask for?"

His snappish remark surprised me. Still, I had to give him some space. God only knew what he'd been through in the past year. Eventually, he'd want to talk about it, and I was prepared to listen.

I went into the house and put on a load of laundry, took a chicken from the freezer, and put it in the refrigerator to thaw. I made a pot of coffee. If Darren didn't want any, I certainly did.

A loud noise from the stairway let me know that the boys were up. They ran into the kitchen. In unison, they asked, "Where is Dad?"

"He's out on the back deck."

"I want to show him my new baseball glove," Connor said.

"And I want him to see the airplane I made," Jeremy chimed in.

They had missed their father so much. Darren was a real dad: taking an interest in everything our sons were involved in. He'd coached Connor's baseball team, been a Cub Scout leader for Jeremy's troop, and he never missed anything they participated in at school.

"Go ahead. I'm sure Daddy will like seeing them." Maybe the boys could snap Darren out of his mood. I followed them, but hung back. I simply observed as they pounced on Darren and began talking, both at the same time.

"Isn't it cool?" Connor asked, shoving the baseball glove into Darren's face.

"Dad, look what I made. I did it all by myself. It can fly, too." Jeremy moved the wooden plane through the air, holding on to it so that Darren could see how well made it was.

"That's nice, Jeremy," Darren said. "And you've got yourself a great glove, Connor. Boys, I'll take a look at your things later, okay? I need to rest right now."

Never, no matter how tired he was, had Darren brushed off the boys. Their faces reflected their disappointment. I told them to come inside for breakfast, hoping a bowl of cereal would take their minds off their dad's indifference.

Though I expected Darren to snap out of his mood, a month after his return, he was still distant. Nothing interested him—including his job.

One afternoon, I came home from work at the county library and found Darren sitting at the table drinking whiskey.

Darren had never been a drinker—maybe a beer now and then, or wine with a special meal, but not whiskey. The look on his face told me that mentioning it wasn't smart, so, like always, I kept my mouth shut.

The phone rang. I answered it. Jack Garnett, the foreman at the factory where Darren worked, was on the line.

"Mrs. Hutton, have you seen Darren, today?"

"Yes. He's right here. Would you like to speak to him?"

"I'd rather talk to you," he said. "Darren didn't come to work today, and he only worked three days last week. I've cut him some slack because he's just back from Iraq, but I need someone I can depend on. He has to come in and do his job, or I'll have no choice but to fire him."

"Fire him! Oh, please, Mr. Garnett, don't do that. My job doesn't pay enough to support us. I'll talk to Darren. I'm sure that once he understands he'll be as reliable as he was before he went to Iraq."

"Make sure he's here tomorrow. This is his last warning." He hung up the phone.

The time for coddling Darren was past. I could put up with his moods, but I couldn't let him lose his job. I went back to the kitchen and sat across from him.

"That was Jack Garnett on the phone," I said. "He tells me you aren't showing up for work. Darren, he's giving you one last chance.

Either you go to work every day, or he's going to fire you."

"Let him," Darren said, pouring another glass of whiskey. "Do you really think I care about that lousy job?"

"Maybe you don't, but the boys and I count on you. Darren, my job doesn't pay enough to take care of the bills."

"Have you ever thought that I might be tired of taking care of the bills? I joined the National Guard because you wanted a bigger house. I stayed in because Connor needed braces, and then you got the idea that Jeremy should go to a private school for gifted children."

"You didn't buy this house just because I needed more room, Darren. We both wanted out of our old neighborhood because of the bad element that moved in. As for Jeremy's school, yes, I wanted it for him. He's gifted, and when he graduates, he can write his own ticket. Ivy League colleges will be offering him full scholarships."

"So I lay my life on the line, and when I come home, nobody wants to give me time to do what I want to do."

My jaw hurt from pressing my teeth so tightly together, holding back bitter words. "What is it you want to do, Darren? All I've you do is sit here with a bottle of booze while you stare into space."

"I knew you'd jump on me about the whiskey!" he shouted. "Cassie, I'm a thirty-two- year old man. If I want to take a drink in my own house, I damn well will!"

It was useless to try to reason with him. "Just tell me one thing, and I'll leave you and your liquor alone. Are you going to work, tomorrow?"

"I'll think about it, tomorrow," he said sarcastically, doing an impression of Scarlett O'Hara.

Disgusted, I walked out of the kitchen and joined the boys in the living room, where they were playing a video game. I stayed until it was time to make dinner. The second I stepped into the kitchen, Darren went outside on the deck. We didn't speak another word to each other that night.

He went to bed first, passed out from drinking. I saw something that gave me hope, though. He'd set his alarm clock. Darren planned to go to work.

The next morning, Darren showered and left for his job. Feeling good for once, I began to hope that everything would work out. I fed the children, and then dropped them off at the community center's summer day care, a few blocks from where I worked.

It was Friday, and we had "Time for Twos" at the library. I was in charge of the group and looked forward to reading and singing with the two-year-olds who attended my session.

I'd been at work about a half hour when I got a phone call. "Mrs. Hutton, this is Deputy Ralph," an unfamiliar voice said. "We need you

66

to come down to the sheriff's office and pick up your husband."

"What happened?"

"He got into a brawl in a bar when the bartender cut him off. He didn't hurt anyone, but he smashed up the place. The bartender isn't going to press charges, but Mr. Hutton will have to pay for the damages."

He hadn't gone to work after all. Instead, he'd gone out drinking, and he'd trashed a bar. This time, he'd gone too far.

"Deputy Ralph, I'm at work and I can't leave. Will you hold him there until I get off at six?"

"Don't you have anyone who can come for him?"

"I don't, but maybe he knows someone. Really, I have to get to work, deputy. You see, Darren no longer has a job. I'm the sole support of my family, now."

My chest ached. How could Darren be so irresponsible? Sure, he'd been to Iraq, and I know it was hard on him, but he hadn't been injured, so why couldn't he put the war out of his mind and concentrate on his family?

After work, I picked up the boys, and then I drove to the sheriff's office. "Stay in the car, and when Daddy comes out, don't say a word."

I went in and was told that Darren's brother-in-law had picked him up a few hours ago. That was fine with me. Now, maybe someone else in the family would see what I'd been going through.

Jordan Rock was married to Darren's oldest sister, Shayna. Jordan had been sent to Vietnam shortly after he and Shayna were married. Maybe he would have some insight into what was going on with Darren. I looked forward to talking to him. Jordan's car was in the drive when I pulled in.

"Boys, go to your rooms, or you can play out back. I need to talk to Uncle Jordan."

They obeyed me, though I could see the confusion on their faces. Once inside, I found Jordan sitting in the living room, waiting for me.

"Darren's sleeping it off," he said.

"Lovely. He destroys our family's financial security, and then he gets to 'sleep it off.' Do you know how much it's going to cost to repay the damage at the bar?"

"It's already been handled. Shayna and I covered it."

"Oh, Jordan, it wasn't your responsibility. I'll pay you back, someway."

He looked shyly down at his shoes. It was a habit he'd had for as long as I'd known him. "Cassie, in a way I feel responsible. If I'd come over more after he got back from Iraq, I might have seen what was going on."

67

"No way are you responsible. This is all Darren's doing."

"War changes people, Cassie. Everyone who goes to war is touched by it in some way. It takes a while to work things out when you come home. Unfortunately, for the soldier, most people think that as long as he made it back alive, he should be able to pick up where he left off."

That was exactly what I'd thought. We would pick up where we left off. We moved from the living room to the kitchen. I fixed iced tea for us, and we sat at the table. Jordan seemed to have aged more than I'd noticed. His forehead was wrinkled, and crow's feet lined his narrowly spaced brown eyes.

"I've been where he is, Cassie," Jordan said. "And it was hell. Back then, we were treated like malingerers if we complained. At least these days, folks are starting to realize that soldiers' problems are real."

"I don't understand," I said.

"Lots of people don't understand. Cassie, get Darren to a doctor. I've seen the same behavior in a lot of men who've gone to wars. This can destroy the man and everyone he loves."

"If he would only talk to me, I think we could work things out," I said.

"That's the thing. Darren can't talk about it. And even if he did, I doubt if you would understand. Cassie, you have to decide something: Your husband fought for America, do you have the guts to fight for him? Are you willing to get him to a psychiatrist? You have to help Darren because he won't help himself. He'd have to face the demons that are haunting him."

"I want to help Darren, but Jordan, how can we afford psychiatric help? If Darren won't work, we'll lose everything."

"That's true. You very well might lose everything. Just decide what matters the most. No one will hold it against you if you want to leave Darren."

His words stung. I'd never imagined leaving Darren. I'd loved him since tenth grade. A woman doesn't leave the love of her life. But was he still the same man I'd fallen so deeply in love with? I honestly didn't know anymore.

How could I be expected to shoulder all the family's burdens? It wasn't fair. Of course, I understood what Jordan was saying. If there were any way in the world to help Darren, I would do it. But I couldn't manufacture money.

"Jordan, is there anything else we can try besides a psychiatrist?"

"There are support groups. Even if Darren won't go, they're available for family members. Cassie, maybe you should go to a couple of meetings. They will help you understand what Darren is going through. It sure can't hurt."

"I've never imagined myself as someone who goes to meetings," I said. "You know my parents and how I was raised. We kept our problems to ourselves, and we dealt with them quietly."

"Your husband was arrested, today. He's been fired from his job. The word is going to get around no matter how much you want to keep it a secret. So why not get some help? You're going to need it if you're going to keep your family together."

Jordan was right, and as much as I hated the idea of airing our dirty laundry in public, I had to get a better understanding of Darren's problem. "Thank-you so much for everything you've done."

"Call me if you need me. Shayna feels the same way. If either of us can help, you know the phone number. I'd better get on home, now."

I saw Jordan to the door. It was late, and I should have gone to bed, but my head was swimming. I wanted to help Darren, but there were other things to consider. Since he had been fired for cause, there would be no unemployment check. My income covered food, utilities, and extra things the boys needed. There was still the house payment, health insurance, car payments, and property taxes.

Without Darren's income, I had to find a way to keep us solvent. The newspaper sat unread on the coffee table. I turned to the want ads and began reading. I only had an associate's degree, and that wouldn't get me into the league of big earnings. I needed something that paid a decent wage and would still let me keep my job at the library.

There was a listing for a job at the factory where Darren had worked. They needed people in the shipping department to work the night shift. I could do it. Darren could stay with the boys at night while I worked.

The light of hope filtered through the end of my agonizingly dark tunnel of fear. I turned off the downstairs lights and went up to bed. Darren was passed out, sleeping off his day of drinking. I showered, and then made my bed on the sofa, unable to endure his drunken stench.

After work the next day, I went to fill out an application at the factory. Darren's old boss saw me and we talked. Once he realized my predicament, he spoke with personnel, and asked them to hire me. I was told to come in the next day at five-thirty. I would work until twelve-thirty.

Darren was watching television with the boys when I got home. He was sober and I was thankful.

"I put in an application for a second job," I told him. "They hired me. The hours worked out great. I get off work at the library at four-thirty, and my next job starts at five-thirty. I can drive the boys' home, change clothes, and be at work on time."

He scowled. "What is this, Cassie? You're trying to play the martyr?"

"I'm trying to give you time to readjust to being home, and I'm also trying to keep a roof over our heads. Darren, you spent a year in living hell, and deserve some time to readjust. I love you, and I want you to have the time you need."

"You think something's wrong with me, don't you?"

"I think you've gone through a difficult year."

"Heck no! You think I've flipped out. Cassie, there is nothing wrong with me. I'm adjusting just fine. The reason I quit working at the factory was that it was a crummy job. I'm thinking about going back to college and finishing my degree. I can get the GI Bill to pay for it."

"That would be wonderful. I'll do anything I can to help you."

"I'll help myself, and I'll stay head of this house, too. I heard some of the guys in my unit talk about how you women got the idea that you wore the pants in the family and wanted to keep things that way."

"I'm not one of those women. I'd be happy to have things exactly as they were before Iraq, but I'm not sitting on my butt and letting our family fall apart as long as I have strength in my body."

He stood, took long strides to the door, and slammed out of the house. I knew where he was going, and I doubted if he'd be back for a long time. I made dinner for the boys and me. Afterward, I set up the sofa so Darren could sleep on it. This time, the bed was mine. I needed as much sleep as I could get.

The next morning, I got ready for work while Darren snored from the sofa. He was sleeping in the same clothes he'd worn the night before, and he hadn't so much as taken his shoes off. As much as I wanted to wake him and yell at him for his self-destructive behavior, I knew I needed to save my energy for the day ahead, so I decided to let him sleep.

I left the library at the end of my shift, picked up the boys from the community center, drove them home, put on a pizza for their dinner, changed, and headed out for my other job. Not once did I see Darren. He was home, but obviously, he was avoiding me.

Work at the factory was hard, but I enjoyed it. The people laughed and joked, unlike in the library where everything was said in whispers. At the end of the shift, I was exhausted. When I reached home, Darren's car was gone. It was the middle of the night.

"Darn you, Darren," I yelled into the dark, empty night. "You left our boys alone!" The boys never had been left alone. They were too young. I hurried to their rooms to check on them. Both were sleeping. A million what-ifs raced through my mind. Anything could have happened to them.

70

As much as I wanted to stay up and have it out with Darren, I needed my rest. I hadn't been feeling well lately; a condition I blamed on stress. In the morning, I'd talk to Darren about his irresponsible behavior.

Darren never came home that night. I hurried the boys through breakfast, drove them to the center, and then went to the library. My nerves were raw. I could barely hold back the tears, and I was so upset that I was dizzy.

"Cassie," Minerva Wells, another assistant, said, "what's the matter? You haven't been yourself for weeks. I don't want to pry, but I'm very worried about you."

I almost, by instinct, said that nothing was wrong. Then I realized that I wanted to talk to someone. Mindy and I went into the ladies' room, and I told her about what had been going on since Darren came home.

"Oh, you poor thing. Isn't there something you can do?"

"If I could do something," I said, "I would have weeks ago. Darren won't go for help. He doesn't even think there is anything wrong with him."

"Then you go for help. The main library lets local organizations use their conference rooms on weekends for meetings. Let's find a group that might be of help to you." Mindy was sweet, and her intentions were good. I had to wonder, though, when she thought I'd have time to go to a meeting. Weekends were for house cleaning.

"You're sweet to think of it," I said, "but I'm so busy on weekends."

Mindy shook her head. "Cassie, you can take an hour for yourself. Isn't it worth it if you learn some way to cope with Darren's problem?"

She was right. "Okay, let's find a group."

We found one, and I called to register for a meeting. All that week, until I was actually at the door to the conference room, I almost backed out. Talking to strangers about intimate family problems terrified me.

As it turned out, I wasn't forced to talk. Instead, I listened. The people were all dealing with a loved one's problems. Some had kids on drugs, others a spouse who drank, or was going through depression. One man talked about his wife, who had been raped a year ago and wouldn't leave the house anymore.

The counselor was a psychologist who competently kept the meeting in hand, encouraging members to offer ideas to the current speaker. Funny, but the ideas didn't mention the troubled teen or the raped wife. The general advice was how we in the group should find ways to cope.

Robert Bacon, the psychiatrist, said something that profoundly touched me. "No one can change anyone. They can only decide how they'll cope with the problem."

"But people do change," a woman said.

"Yes, they do," Dr. Bacon said. "When they decide they want to change and reach out for help, then they will. But no one else can make it happen. You, in this group, are the survivors of their behavior. To learn to survive is why we're here."

After the meeting, I managed to get a few minutes with Dr. Bacon. I spilled my guts about Darren. Dr. Bacon listened intently, and then said, "I'm going to be in my office at five to see a little girl who was sexually abused. If you will come there at six, I'd be glad to talk about your husband's problem with you."

For once, there was no hesitation. "I'll see you at six."

At six, I found myself in his office, complaining about everything Darren had done since coming back from the war. Dr. Bacon took notes, and asked questions. He wanted to meet Darren.

"He'll never come," I said. "Darren can't admit anything's wrong with him."

"I think he admits it to himself every day," Dr. Bacon said. "I've treated men who've come home from wars. You can't imagine what these men go through."

"No, but I do know what an alcoholic is, and Darren is becoming one."

"Your husband isn't drinking because he's addicted to alcohol, Cassie. He's drinking to numb his brain so he won't think of the horrors that haunt him. Post-traumatic stress disorder can be a lingering, and terribly misunderstood illness."

"But everyone has stress," I said.

"This is a different kind of stress. It comes from witnessing something terrible, or from being raped, mugged, or kidnapped. Child abuse can cause it. It shocks the nervous system and leaves the victim numb, unable to show affection, or to cope in social or work situations."

Dr. Bacon sounded as though he were describing Darren. "Can I help Darren?"

"If you do, you'll become codependent. He'll never get the help he really needs."

I left the office more confused than before. Now, I understood that Darren was sick. And I also realized that if I tried to help him, I'd eliminate the need for him to reach out and see Dr. Bacon.

Darren was home with the boys when I came in. "Where have you been, Cassie? It's after seven."

"Out," I said.

"I'd like an explanation."

"Darren, anytime I ask where you've been, you say 'out.' Well, I've been out. Have you and the boys had dinner?"

"We snacked. I figured you'd be home soon and make dinner, or at least bring something from a fast-food joint."

"Darren, I worked sixteen hours a day this past week. I woke up at six this morning and washed clothes. I even cooked breakfast and lunch before I left. Tomorrow, I'll clean the house, cook three meals, and do everything else that needs to be done. It seems like you could have made sandwiches for you and the boys."

"That's lovely, Cassie. I come back from fighting a war, and you're not even willing to make me something to eat."

"You've been back from the war for almost two months, and you haven't turned your hand to take any responsibility for your home and family. Darren, you left the boys alone to go out drinking the other night."

"What's the big deal? They were asleep. You pamper them too much."

"If social services learned that they were left alone, they could take the boys from us and put them in a foster home. What you did was negligent."

"Oh, I so do not need the drama queen bit. Give me some money."

"Why?"

"I don't have any cash."

"Sorry. I can't afford to make contributions to the local bars. Guess you'll be staying home, tonight."

He looked at me as though he wanted to slap me. I stood my ground. Every day, he asked for money, and I'd given it to him because I didn't want him to think I was taking over his role as head of the house.

"Darren, the money I earn is for the benefit of our family, and your blowing it on booze doesn't benefit anyone—especially you. Besides, I'm going to need the money to pay the doctor."

"Doctor? Are you sick?"

"Yes. And so are the boys. We're sick and tired of the way you ignore us and won't even try to get help for your problems."

"I don't have any problems."

"Right. You give them to everybody else, while you crawl into a bottle of whiskey. I'm seeing a psychologist, and I'm going to take the boys. We love you, and we have to have some way to express our frustrations because we can't talk to you."

He slammed out of the room, knocking things over, cursing, and calling me the worse names imaginable. I heard our bedroom door close with a loud bang.

Over the next three weeks, nothing changed with Darren, except that he'd stopped wanting sex and had sold his hunting rifles so that he'd have money for liquor. Dr. Bacon was a huge help to the boys and me, but no matter how good his advice was, it didn't change things at home.

Understanding is one thing. Dealing with a matter is something else. I was exhausted, and the dizzy spells had gotten worse. Sleeping was hard. If Darren wasn't out, he was planted in front of the television all night. The TV set was right below our bedroom, and the volume kept me awake. I'd ask him to turn it down, and he would. Then, just as I'd doze off to sleep, I'd hear it again.

Darren had been home three months when I began to doubt that I still loved him. I wanted to love him; actually, I wanted to love the man he'd been before. The man living with me now was a stranger— and not someone I would have picked for a husband. I begged him to come to sessions with Dr. Bacon, but each time, he became angry and threatening.

It was raining the night that everything came to a head. At work that night, I'd felt dizzy and my stomach cramped horribly. I didn't ask to leave work early because we needed the money so badly. One of the other workers pointed out to our foreman that I didn't look well.

"Cassie," the foreman said, "why don't you clock out? Go home; get some rest. We'll still be here, tomorrow."

"I'm okay." There were only three more hours to go.

"Okay, but I don't want you lifting anything heavy. You can schedule shipments until it's time to knock off."

When my time was up, I drove through the miserable rain to the house. Both boys were asleep on the living room floor. Empty soda and beer cans were scattered next to bags of potato chips. The television blared, and Darren was nowhere to be found. His car was in the drive, though, so he couldn't have gone far. I shook Connor to wake him. He opened his eyelids slowly. "Hi, Mom."

"Why are you and your brother sleeping here instead of upstairs in your beds? You both have school, tomorrow."

"We got scared," he said. "Dad went to get some more beer and told us he'd be back in fifteen minutes, but he didn't come back, and it was storming. We were afraid, so we came down here. Sorry about the mess. Dad said he'd clean it up before you got home."

"I'm not concerned about the mess. Connor, your dad's car is here. How could he have gone anywhere?"

"Called a cab. His car battery was dead, so he called a cab to pick him up and take him to the store."

Liquor store was my first guess. "How long ago?"

Connor looked at the clock over the television. "Three hours."

74

"Get your brother and both of you go upstairs to your room." Connor did as he was told, and I began cleaning up the living room. The stomach cramps had gotten worse. I went to the bathroom and saw that I was bleeding.

Taking the blood to be the start of my period, I didn't worry about it very much. I was past due, but it was no big thing since I'd never been regular. After taking care of myself, I returned to cleaning.

This was the last straw for me. I'd done my best to cope with Darren, but now his problem was affecting the safety of our sons. Tomorrow, Darren would see Dr. Bacon, or he would leave and I'd file for divorce.

My cramps became worse. I took three aspirins and stretched out on the sofa. The dizzy feeling came back. Suddenly, the room began to grow black. I felt as though I were floating away. A hard, aching cramp pulled me back.

I struggled to my feet, intending to go to the bathroom, when a gush of blood flooded from me. Something was wrong. This was not a normal period. I needed help. Darren wasn't there, and the boys were too young to help me. I called Shayna and Jordan. No sooner were the words out of my mouth when Shayna said she and Jordan were on their way.

It was fortunate that I'd called them when I had. A few seconds later, I lost consciousness. When I woke, I was being prepped for surgery. Shayna was with me. "The boys?" I whispered.

"Jordan took them to your parents."

My parents lived an hour's drive from us. "They'll miss school."

Shayna laughed. "Girl, after everything you've been through, school should be the least of your worries."

"What do you mean, what I've been through?"

She looked as though she wished she'd never opened her mouth. "They'll know more after the surgery."

"Is Darren here?"

"Jordan's out looking for him. Don't worry about Darren. Try to rest, Cassie. I'll go outside where I can use my cellular and call Jordan to see if he's had any luck finding Darren."

I was taken into surgery before Shayna came back. The next time I awoke, I was in the recovery room. Darren was there. He looked horrible, and he smelled as though he'd fallen into a whiskey barrel.

"You're going to be fine," he said. His voice had absolutely no emotion. He could have been talking to a total stranger for all the concern he showed.

"No, she isn't going to be fine," Shayna said. I hadn't seen her, at first, because she was behind Darren. "Cassie has been through hell, Darren, and you should have been here with her."

"Hey, Shayna, give me a break. Besides, I'm not a doctor. What could I have done?"

"If she hadn't called us when she did, she would be dead by now," Shayna snapped at him. "Darren, Jordan has made me promise not to say anything to you, but you're my brother, and I'm going to break that promise. Since you've been back, you've been a self-centered horse's ass. You ignore the boys and won't turn your hand to help Cassie. No wonder she lost the baby."

Baby? What baby? I thought the drugs were making me hallucinate.

"Shayna, we didn't need another kid, anyway!" Darren yelled. "So give it a rest and get off my back."

"Was I pregnant?" I asked Shayna.

She nodded. "Not quite two months. Honey, you had a hard time, but the doctors feel certain you'll be able to have more children."

"We don't need more children," Darren said. "Look, I need to get out of here."

"Don't go," I pleaded. "Darren, I miscarried our baby. I need you with me."

"You have doctors, nurses, and Shayna. You don't need me."

"Yes I do. I've needed you for over a year. When you came home, I thought everything would be like it was before, but it isn't."

Darren stepped away and leaned against the green wall. "I'm not going to be hounded by you, and I'm not going to stay here so that Shayna can lay a guilt trip on me. So you had a miscarriage? Big deal! It happens all the time."

"Don't you care? Doesn't it matter to you that our baby died?"

He walked out of the room. I tired to get out of the bed. We were going to finish one conversation if I had to crawl on hands and knees to get to him. Shayna wrestled me back into the bed, and a nurse gave me a shot to calm me down.

I was in the hospital three days. After I returned home, Shayna came over to fix meals and help me until I was back on my feet. Darren basically avoided me, as though seeing me made him uncomfortable.

"Kick him out," Shayna said. "Cassie, you've been a saint for putting up with him this long. I know a good divorce lawyer."

Her advice stunned me. She was Darren's sister, yet her advice was exactly what I'd been thinking about since the day Darren stormed out of the post-op room. He hadn't visited me once, or even called to see how I was. My mother said he hadn't checked on the boys, either.

"Shayna, find him and tell him I need to discuss a few things with him. And when he gets here, lock us in this room, even if you have to shove furniture against the door. He's not leaving until we've made some decisions."

76

Finding Darren required Shayna to call every bar in town, without success. I wondered if he was seeing another woman. It wasn't until he made his way home to hit me up for money that I saw him.

"I'll give you the money, if you'll sit down and talk to me for ten minutes. I have something to say. I'm not going to yell or try to give you a guilt trip."

"Can you make it fast?" he asked.

"Sure. Darren, I want you out of here. I'm going to sell the house and file for divorce. I'll find an apartment close to Shayna and Jordan. Shayna promised to watch the boys when I'm working." "You can't kick me out of my own house."

"Have it your way," I said. "Pay me for my share of the house, and the boys and I will move out as soon as I'm able. I plan to file for divorce this week."

"I'm not giving you a divorce," he said. "Cassie, I can't make it without you and the boys."

My temper flared. "That is total bull. What you can't make it without is my support. You don't want to lose your cash cow. Darren, I miscarried and nearly bled to death, and you didn't care. You constantly leave the boys at home alone; so don't try to convince me you love them, either. We're getting out of this disaster before it destroys our sons."

"I'll fight you."

"Great. That means you're going to get a job, because lawyers don't come cheap."

"You have everything figured out, don't you? Fine, I'm leaving." He took a suitcase and packed it haphazardly with underwear, jeans, and some shirts. "I'll get the rest, later."

And he left. I felt a mixed sense of hurt and relief. I'd reached the point where I couldn't go on with Darren. As strong as my love for him had been, it couldn't defeat the demons that he refused to deal with.

After I was well again, I found an apartment in a perfect location. It was a three bedroom, with a nice, sunny kitchen, and a suitable living room. There were washer and dryer connections, too. Everything we needed to get by.

Shayna drove the boys to school and picked them up afterward. Most nights, I'd have dinner with the boys, Shayna, and Jordan, and then go home to change for my factory job.

"Cassie, why don't you quit one of those jobs?" Jordan asked

"I still have bills to pay. I'm covering the mortgage on the house and the rent on the apartment, as well as paying for two cars."

"Why don't you let them foreclose on the house and repossess Darren's car?"

"Not until the divorce. And I don't want to ruin my credit. Darren hasn't responded to the divorce papers, yet. He won't even talk to my lawyer. I've done everything I can to make Darren respond." It was true; I'd had the phone turned off, and the utilities transferred. I also saved money by ending my sessions with Dr. Bacon. With Darren out of my life, I no longer needed him.

As the weeks passed, I kept Darren out of my thoughts as much as possible. Then, when I least expected it, he called me at the library.

"Cassie, can we have dinner, Saturday?" he asked. "Just the two of us. I think we need to talk."

"I can do that," I said. "Where shall I meet you?"

"I'm a gentleman, despite past behavior, and I'd prefer to pick you up at your apartment."

We pleasantly said good-bye and hung up. I began to feel jittery, unable to imagine what Darren wanted to talk about. Probably, he was unhappy with my lawyer's proposed settlement.

When Saturday rolled around, my nerves were as raw as freshly caught fish. My emotions flip-flopped between giddiness and fear. Then it was time for Darren to pick me up. Five minutes passed, then ten, and I wondered if he'd decided not to come.

Just as I kicked off my shoes, certain that Darren wasn't going to keep out date, the bell rang. I put my shoes on and hurried to the door. Darren stood there looking like the man I'd loved for so many years. He was neatly dressed in a suit and tie, shaven, and his hair had been cut.

"Cassie, you look so pretty," he said.

"You look good, too. How have you been?"

"I'm not drinking anymore, and I have a job. That's one of the things I wanted to talk to you about. I can take over the mortgage and car payments."

We left the apartment and went to dinner. The restaurant was intimate and made it easy to carry on a conversation. Darren asked about the boys and I filled him in on how they were doing in school. He wanted to see them, so we arranged for him to come over the next day and spend time with them.

As our meal drew to an end, Darren grew quiet. "Is something wrong?" I asked.

"Cassie, I'm trying to get up the nerve to tell you something."

Oh, no, I thought, he's going to tell me he's found someone else. But why does that matter? I am divorcing him.

He lowered his head, as though he were ashamed. His lips trembled. "I'm so sorry about the baby. I acted like a jerk. Cassie, since I came home from the war I've been like a zombie. Like all of my emotions had been ripped out of me."

I wished he hadn't brought up the baby. It was the one thing that

I couldn't forgive him for. "Let's not discuss the baby."

"Cassie, Robert Bacon is treating me for post-traumatic stress disorder," he blurted out. "Dr. Bacon is treating me free as long as I show up and participate in a group of other soldiers who have the same problem. He helped me get a job, and he's helping me deal with the reason I have the disorder in the first place."

"I'm glad Dr. Bacon is able to help you. I wish you'd have talked about your problems with me when you first came home."

"I couldn't. Talking about it was like reliving what happened. Dr. Bacon forced me to talk about it, and he said that I owe it to you and the boys to tell you what caused my disorder. Could we go back to your place for privacy's sake?"

We drove to the apartment and went inside. I put on a pot of decaf and joined Darren in the living room. He looked pale, and there were beads of sweat on his forehead. After a few seconds of preparing himself, he began the story.

"Our unit was patrolling the streets. There had been some incidents of sniper fire in the area. They'd shot military personnel and civilians. Everything was normal until a car bomb went off a couple of blocks from where some of us were posted. The order came to check it out and offer assistance to anyone injured.

"Randy, Dean, Sean, and I ran the two blocks to help. Other soldiers had already arrived. The car was a burnt out wreck, and the driver lay dead on the street. His body parts were. . . . Cassie, I don't want to go into details so use your imagination."

I wasn't so sure I wanted to use my imagination. It sounded perfectly dreadful. "I'm sure it was traumatic to see."

He smiled a half smile and shook his head. "Honey, that wasn't the cause of my problem. It was what came later. We were checking to see if anyone else had been injured when I heard gunfire and turned around in time to see Smith fall to the ground, clutching his stomach. I knelt beside him and rolled him over. Where the bullet exited had left a gaping hole."

I knew there were things he was holding back so I would be spared the ugly details. And yet, I could imagine Darren as he dealt with the gore.

"How horrible," I said. "Did the man die?"

"Yes. It was a slow, painful death. But that wasn't the end of it. The sniper began picking off soldiers one by one. We wanted to return fire, but didn't know where the sniper was, so we held our fire so that we wouldn't risk hitting civilians. Several times, we called for help—only to be told that the rest of our unit was pinned down by another sniper."

You must have been terrified."

"I thought that any minute I would be killed, but I had to do my duty and see to my fellow soldiers. I dragged Sean behind a vendor's cart that had been knocked over in the blast, and then went to help the other wounded. We were pinned down, with men dying, for an hour before help reached us.

"Robert Bacon told me that a traumatizing event, such as that one, could trigger a chemical reaction that leads to post-traumatic stress. I'm taking medication, and my sessions with Dr. Bacon, as well as the group sessions, are helping me deal."

I believed that Robert Bacon knew what he was doing, and I didn't doubt that the medication was helping Darren, but I still wasn't confident enough to trust that Darren's current improvement was going to last.

"Cassie, would you come to sessions with me? Before we sign the divorce papers, I'd like to give us one last chance. We don't have to live together, but I'd like to include you in my sessions to help you understand why I've been the way I have. The drinking, for instance—I didn't want the whiskey because I liked it. Sleep was impossible, and the nightmares were worse. If I got drunk enough I'd pass out, and most of the time, when I was passed out, I didn't dream."

Before, when the boys and I were seeing Dr. Bacon, I remembered him saying something to that effect. If my going to sessions with Darren would help him, it was the least I could do.

"I'll go, Darren, but understand, I'm not going to be lured back into a bad marriage."

I got us two cups of coffee, and we drank them at the kitchen table. Darren asked more questions about the boys, and I filled him in on everything I could think of just to keep the conversation off us. When time came for him to leave, he shyly kissed my cheek.

Trust, once lost, is the hardest thing in the world to get back. Love, though, is a great healer. Because of the love that still lived in our hearts, Darren and I worked with Robert Bacon in hopes of saving our marriage.

Darren, so determined to prove to me that he was a changed man, kept his job, working at night for a bank, doing data entry. He did so well he was given a promotion. He'd also started taking classes for a degree in business. The drinking stopped, too. And he never missed one of the boys' school events or ball games.

I won't lie and say that everything was perfect, because it wasn't. A person suffering from Darren's disorder requires a long time to heal. He dealt with nightmares, panic attacks, and sometimes he would shut himself off because he couldn't cope. A song, or a movie—even seeing someone who resembled one of the men who were killed—could send his mind reeling back to that dark place.

Patience and love, if the love is real, go hand in hand. It took us four months of counseling before I felt confident enough to move back to our house. The boys had wanted to go home after their first weekend with Darren, but I had to be certain it was going to work before uprooting them again.

When we did go home, I found myself feeling shy with Darren. Inside, I couldn't erase all that had happened and jump into bed with him. But Darren was considerate and patient. Soon, we became a real married couple, again—in every sense of the word.

Post-traumatic stress disorder is a demon set to destroy innocent lives. With the right kind of help, and a heaping dose of love, it can be vanquished. Sometimes, from deep inside its victim, it will sneak out. That is when loved ones must work the hardest to understand and be patient. After Darren's experience, I came to believe stronger than ever in the saying, "Love conquers all."

THE END

THE U.S. SOLDIER
EVERY WOMAN WANTS!
He's overseas, but I want him over me!

For years I watched them fall in love—my best friend, Susie, and her boyfriend, Ethan. I guess you could call Ethan my other best friend. Ethan and I always had a lot in common. We were both good at math in school. We both loved motorcycles. And we were both crazy about Susie.

That's why everything seems so weird now.

And what if Susie changes her mind? And how did she know? But that's Susie for you, always seeing something that Ethan and I missed, always being good-hearted about things. She's been like that ever since we were kids.

Susie was one of those unusual girls—beautiful, popular, and genuinely nice to everybody. She and Ethan had known each other all their lives. They were childhood playmates, growing up practically next door to each other in our little town of Camden. My family moved to Camden around the start of middle school. I'll never forget those first, tough weeks as the new girl in school, and Susie reaching out to me. I was sitting in the cafeteria feeling invisible when this pretty girl with braids came to my empty table and sat down by me.

"What's your name?" she asked me, smiling.

"Tara," I answered.

"Oh, you are so lucky to have such a beautiful name!"

And at that first kindness, I became Susie's devoted friend for life.

Susie was outgoing and I was shy. Susie was sure there was sunshine around every corner and I was wondering where the next slap was coming from. I'll never know why she and Ethan took me under their wings. We all just hit it off. Soon Susie, Ethan, and I were a threesome.

We saw each other in school, after school, and on weekends. We hung out, went to the pool, watched TV, and did our homework together. We talked about our dreams. With Ethan it was motorcycles. He wanted to buy them, ride them, own them, and fix them, anything so long as it was motorcycles. Susie counseled that it was a good hobby, but he should go to college and get a great job so that he could buy all the motorcycles he wanted. Susie wanted to be a doctor, or a model, or sometimes a teacher. Looking back, out of the three of us, she had the most imagination, the most ability to see herself in places beyond quiet, little Camden. I wanted to be a nurse. Ever since I was in the hospital with appendicitis when I was ten, that's all I ever wanted to do. I also thought I'd be in heaven if I could ride a motorcycle to work.

It's good to tell friends about your dreams. Friends believe in you. They can see you getting to where you want to go, and this helps you. Most kids get this kind of help with future plans from their parents, but in my case it was Ethan and Susie who could see me as a success. At home I was just another kid in a house with too many kids. The thought that I might want to go to college had not yet occurred to my parents. And I did not discuss my dreams at home. But with Ethan and Susie, I was always making plans.

What I remember most from those years is just hanging out at Susie's house. Susie's mom was always cooking, and her dad liked to build things. She had a couple of brothers who seemed to be forever dribbling basketballs through the house. Susie's mother was funny, and she had a million rules that made life there interesting. For example, dribbling was allowed, but throwing hoop shots indoors was strictly forbidden.

There's another thing I remember. There was always enough supper for extra guests. And they ate dessert. Susie's mother made pies, assembly line style. She would grab one of her big sons as they dribbled by, tie an apron on him, and make him help. He would yell that it was a violation of child labor laws. She would put a spoonful of pie filling in his mouth. They would laugh. The pies were always delicious.

This was so different from my house that I thought I'd landed in a foreign country—a nice foreign country where it was okay to be a kid.

My house would have made an interesting reality show. My mother acted like the world had done her wrong. She was pretty once, but all that's left of her former beauty is a certain toss of her head, when she was feeling really good. She's not a bad person, don't get me wrong. She's just someone who sees the glass as half-empty, and she always felt she deserved a refill.

Dad, when he was around, would refill the glass with dark, amber alcohol. They both preferred to see the world through a haze of alcohol and cigarette smoke. My dad was generally a sweet guy who couldn't seem to make much money, but he could be a mean drunk, and then my mother would cry. I have three brothers, one younger than me and two older. Early on, we kids learned to fend for ourselves. My older brothers got in trouble and they both went to juvenile detention centers. My oldest brother is in prison now. My younger brother missed a lot of the chaos because my parents got clean and sober when he was around five years old. I was in high school by then, spending as much time as possible out of the house and away with my friends.

That's about when hormones started kicking in for all of us. When Susie and Ethan started having sex, things changed. I recognized this, and I was careful to respect their new closeness. Fortunately, through all these changes, the continuity was our ongoing friendship, a sense that we all cared about each other no matter what. We still did a lot of things together but Ethan often brought along a friend as date for me.

They were all good guys, but none of those little romances lasted. You see, Ethan and Susie were the great loves of my life. I needed them. Looking at them, I could see that love was a happy thing. And they needed me, too. I'm not exactly sure what for, but they liked having me around. Susie and I were like sisters. Neither one of us had a sister, so maybe that's why we got along really well. And Ethan bossed us around, and teased and protected us both. Maybe their love needed a third person to watch it happen and appreciate it, to prove to them that it was real. Who knows? I just know it felt right when we were all together, and we had some great times.

Susie's family was very active in their church, and we all went to her youth group events and once in awhile to church. I was never very interested in church, but I was curious. People seemed to get so much enjoyment from it. I felt like an outsider, watching a play. But it was a sincere sort of play, and I loved the music. We went with Susie to youth group all through high school, and took some nice trips and did community service projects. Susie and I joined a little singing group that visited the local hospital and the nursing homes around Christmas time. I still remember the feeling of singing those songs, my voice a steady alto, ebbing smoothly beneath Susie's floating soprano voice.

High school ended and Susie and I went to nursing school. I was thrilled that she decided to do that with me. It made me feel like I'd made the right choice, like I was the one with answers about life for a change. Ethan tried college, but he was just a very restless guy in those days and he dropped out after a year. He went into the army, and soon he was in Iraq. Susie and I wrote him lots of letters, and sent funny packages and emails. Susie was wild with excitement when he was due to come home on a short leave.

I came home from the grocery store one day just in time to hear her message, as I was coming through the door.

"Well, he's back!" Susie's happy voice told my answering machine.

A few days later, however, Susie sounded sad. "He's different," she told me as we sipped coffee on our break at Camden General Hospital, where we both found work after nursing school.

"Well, sure, he would be. Give it time."

"No, I mean he's really different."

84

I tried to think what would help. "Hey, let's all go out for supper tonight. We could go to Memory Lane, like old times."

Memory Lane is a bar and restaurant where everybody in town congregates sooner or later. They have old-fashioned jukeboxes, affordable prices, and great meals. Back in high school, Susie's parents took us all there for Susie's sixteenth birthday. We went there for dinner before the prom. We went there when we got old enough to order a drink legally. Ethan took us there to celebrate our new jobs at the hospital, and we took Ethan there when he came home from basic training. The plastic grapevines and the red and white checked tablecloths were as familiar and comforting as home.

"Okay, that's a good idea, but you ask him."

I was glad to. Ever since Susie and Ethan had become intimate, I'd backed off from Ethan. It just made things simpler, safer. I didn't want to disturb the closeness they had, or even appear to. So, with Susie's blessing, I was happy to call Ethan's dad's house and ask to speak to my hero.

"Tara! How are you? How's everything?" His voice sounded wonderfully the same. Ethan agreed to be kidnapped for dinner. "Your letters and the packages were wonderful. I traded the magic markers for foot powder. And the chocolate melted a dozen times before it got to me, but we ate it all anyway." Soon Ethan and I were laughing and joking just as we always had.

Memory Lane was pleasantly noisy with clattering dishes and groups of friends. We sat at our favorite booth. It was sheltered by woodsy potted plants, but had a wide-angle view of the dining room. Lots of people recognized Ethan and came over to shake his hand and talk. Ethan seemed the same to me. He was full of talk, turning hardships into entertaining stories. It was Susie who was strangely quiet, not quite her carefree self.

Susie and I worked the same twelve-hour shifts, so we both had three days off coming up. I knew those two lovebirds would be together, and I knew I needed to keep busy. I was fighting my old attraction to Ethan, which I'd always kept very private. It was true, Ethan was my hero as far as guys went. These feelings would lie underground most of the time, and then something would trigger them and I'd want more attention from him, and then I'd start to feel a little jealous of Susie. I never liked myself when this happened. I knew it was wrong to want my best friend's boyfriend and that I was probably just insecure. But no other man on the planet appealed to me. I had tried going out with other guys. There were a few sparks, but no deep, laughing friendships ever developed to fan those little flames.

With Ethan home, I tried hard not to think about them being together. I knew I had to find a project to occupy me. I decided to paint my apartment. I was thinking about it for a while, envisioning the pale peach and light coral tints I wanted in my three sunny, upstairs rooms. My landlady, Mrs. Pembroke, was fine with it. She told me to go ahead and paint however I wanted to. I guess she trusted my decorating skills. I moved all the furniture into the middle of the rooms and got going. Soon I lost myself in my favorite music and the rhythm of the paint roller. I practiced old ballet steps as I reached and brushed, spreading pale, peach paint on every wall.

This little apartment is the first home of my own I've ever had. My family moved around a lot when I was a kid, so having a place of my own is a big deal to me. From the moment I moved in, Susie and Ethan teased me about it. They called it my dollhouse. They're right. This is where my "control freak" nature reigns. There is a place for everything and—you know the rest. This is where I keep everything special to me, and where I go to rest up so that I can deal with the world.

During those days off, I played my favorite CDs over and over again, and painted until I was exhausted. By the last night, my curtains were back up and the whole place was fresh with the smell of paint and cleanser. I looked around in satisfaction at the warm, inviting rooms, reflecting soft, coral light.

Back at work the next day, Susie was so quiet and pale that I was instantly concerned. When we took our break, I squeezed Susie's arm and asked her what was wrong.

"Ethan and I have decide to be . . . just friends," Susie said carefully.

"Oh, honey," was all I could say. I was shocked. I didn't see this coming at all. I didn't try to hug Susie. I could tell that it might make her fall apart. Plus, I was trying to squash my totally disloyal reaction, my hope that now maybe Ethan would pay more attention to me. Maybe Ethan would stop seeing me as Susie's shadow and take me more seriously. But that wasn't really fair. Ethan already took me seriously. We were friends.

"It's okay," said Susie. "It's better, really. You know what, Tara? It's not Ethan who's different. It's me. He's ready to . . . you know, settle down when he comes back home next year and I'm just getting started. I want to travel and I want to work in a big hospital and maybe go back to school."

"Are you sure about this?" I asked. I still couldn't process that they'd broken up. More likely it was just a spat and they would kiss and make up by evening, just like they used to. They were both stubborn and had often had spats, but they always got back together.

"No," Susie admitted. "But I think it's the right thing to do right now."

"How's Ethan doing?" I asked. I was curious.

"Oh, he's pretty mad." We both smiled at that. We were both familiar with Ethan's quick temper. It flared up when he didn't get his own way, or when he was confronted with something that he didn't understand.

"But he knows I'm right," Susie added.

This I could imagine, too. Ethan had always been a strong boy, seeking physical solutions for things. Then his mom got really sick, and he had to help watch out for his little brothers while his father worked. As he was plunged into these family cares, his heart seemed to grow into his big, muscular body. He still got mad when things didn't go his way, but he could laugh at himself, too, and he listened. I always loved that about him; he listened. Well, to be honest, I loved everything about him.

Soon Ethan was back in Iraq. I didn't get to see him before he left. Maybe that was just as well. I could be close with Susie, or I could fantasize about Ethan, but it was too confusing to feel both ways at the same time. In the meantime I would concentrate on being a friend to Susie. She was tough, though. She closed up and got very private and very determined. I'd never seen her like that before.

Well, maybe I have. I remembered when we were about eleven and she wanted a horse. Her parents explained that though she had a great idea there and it would be really nice, they just couldn't fit it into the family budget. I thought that was pretty cool of them to explain their answer, instead of just telling her no, it was a dumb idea, like my parents would've. But Susie was undeterred. She decided to earn the money to buy a horse anyway. She babysat, she mowed lawns, and she even got a paper route. She saved her money for about three years.

By the time she'd earned enough money, she didn't really care so much about having a horse anymore, but she started to get interested in medicine. I guess hearing me talk constantly about my part-time job at the hospital had an effect. She started taking a nurse's aide course with me, and pretty soon we were both planning to go to the local community college that had a nursing program.

She was much better at it than I was. Susie has always had such a heart full of love for the patients. I was good at the educational part, the math and the memorization. Together we got through all those hard courses, and our clinical placements. Finally it was time to graduate, and take the state nursing boards.

It was sheer luck that we both got jobs at Camden General Hospital. The nursing shortage was just beginning to be felt in our area. Several nurses had left our little hospital because they were retiring, or taking higher paying jobs elsewhere. That opened up some positions at Camden General. Susie felt it was a good job to have while she waited for Ethan to get out of the Army. For me, it was my big dream come true. I just loved it, the structure, the uniforms, the patients—everything. I even liked the paperwork. I liked the precision of nursing and the sense of order. Susie loved taking care of the people, the patients. But after Ethan went back to Iraq, I noticed that she was quieter and less interested in what went on at the hospital.

So I shouldn't have been so shocked when she decided to take another job in a big teaching hospital a hundred miles away, but I was. It really seemed to perk her up, though, and she was more like the Susie I knew, so I was happy for her. We talked a lot as I helped her pack and helped her move and then helped her unpack in her new place. We talked about everything under the sun except Ethan. That was a closed door. If I brought him up, she gently but firmly changed the subject.

Now both of my friends were far away. I missed them. I wrote them both cheerful letters. It was kind of a reflective time for me. Suddenly, I was alone. Camden was home to me, but none of my family lived there anymore. To my parents, this town had been just another theater where they acted out their complicated, unhappy marriage. Sobriety may have forestalled chronic liver disease, but it did not seem to have healed anything else. They had divorced and gone their separate ways a few years before. There was my little brother, still in high school, but he had moved away with my mom.

"Move up here with me, Tara. It's fun," urged Susie. "There are tons of jobs here."

I tried to think about moving. I remembered being "new" every time my parents decided to move when I was a kid. I thought about my patients at the hospital—our high school English teacher who was in for bypass surgery, my neighbor's child with those bad asthma attacks, and the man who ran the newspaper store, who needed chemotherapy.

Moving had always been hard for me. I wanted to stay put for a while. Maybe I was just lazy, but I wanted to stay where I knew my way around, and where I already knew some people. Camden was home. I loved the change of seasons. I loved my job. Some days I would ask myself if this was what I really wanted to do with my life. And a soft voice deep in my heart would answer: Yes.

"I want to stay here," I said simply. Susie nodded, understanding. She remembered how I felt about being the new kid in school. That's what's so great about Susie. She knew the painful places in my heart, and she respected them. That's partly why, all through high school, I had practically lived at Susie's house. I wanted to have Susie's life with Susie's family. Her family was amazing, right off the cover of a magazine. And it was real. I spent as much time there as possible.

It comforted me to go there and see the same family photos on the same mantle year after year. There was even one with Ethan and me in it, our double date the night of the prom. It was an eight by twelve with Ethan, tall and handsome with his arm around Susie, and my date standing next to me, though I can barely remember his name. It didn't matter what his name was because his name wasn't Ethan.

I visited Susie in her new place. She was right. It was fun. We would shop and go to movies or just loll around her apartment talking until all hours. I loved visiting her in the city. Still, I was always glad to come home to my own sunny apartment, to my plants, to my life in one place. Visiting Susie reminded me of that old children's story about the country mouse and the city mouse. I decided that come spring, I would plant a garden and sink my fingers a little deeper into the soil of Camden.

I don't remember having plants or gardens around when I was growing up, but Susie's mother has two green thumbs. She taught me a lot about plants, about taking cuttings and transplanting and all that. My apartment is full of plants, mostly cuttings I've gotten from her. She told me the secret of growing plants is that they don't like to be ignored. Forget fertilizer, she said. All you have to do is pay attention to them, she said, and they flourish.

At first, after Ethan went back to Iraq, I wrote him lots of cheery, friendly letters. But as the months went by with no letters coming back, I thought maybe I was making it awkward for him. Maybe he was totally preoccupied with wanting to get back with Susie. There was another possibility and I had to face it: Maybe he just didn't want to be friends anymore.

The snow melted. Susie's phone calls were full of excitement. She was dating someone new, a guy she met at a church medical conference. She was talking about how much she was learning, and getting a promotion. Meanwhile, I was reading books about gardening and telling her all about tomatoes, onions, and forget-me-nots.

"That's a funny combination," teased Susie, in one of our long, late-night phone calls. Maybe, I thought to myself, but maybe not. Forget-me-nots because I love their brave, little blue faces. And tomatoes for sauce in the fall when Ethan will be home again, this time for good.

Susie's mother taught me to cook. Many afternoons, I would sit on a stool in her kitchen and watch, or help her chop and stir, as she prepared supper. Spaghetti sauce was one of her specialties. She made it with tomatoes from her garden, and onions and garlic chopped very fine, and spices by the spoonful. During high school, Ethan and I were at Susie's house for supper more often than we were at our own homes. Ethan liked to hang around with Susie's mom, too. Ethan liked her spaghetti, I remembered.

Ethan. I couldn't keep him out of my mind. I wanted him to turn to me so that I could help him heal his broken heart. Then he would forget Susie, fall in love with me, and we would live happily ever after. I did feel a little funny fantasizing about him, knowing as much as I did about his sex life with Susie. How would I like it if he were touching me and thinking about her? I didn't care, I decided, just as long as he touched me. Susie was my best friend in the whole world. But I wanted her ex-boyfriend and I wanted him now. I knew this was pretty mixed up, and I felt odd writing to him when I got no replies, so I decided to stop writing. I didn't want to lose hold on reality completely. And being lovers with Ethan was not reality. At least not right then, and probably it never would be.

Months dragged by and I forced myself to think of other things. I planted my garden. I took a soap-making class at the community college. I was getting very good at the new computer patient records system at the hospital. Spring opened up a summer of hot days and bright blue skies. I forced myself to have a life without my friends.

So I was astonished when Ethan called me. He was home. He'd been home a few days, he said. He invited me to go to Memory Lane with him. The restaurant was cozy and familiar, but I had to accept that this time Ethan really was different, nervous and fidgety, and his face was tight and serious. Finally, I put my hand on his tanned arm.

"Ethan, relax. It's me, Tara. Remember?"

He turned to face me and cleared his throat. "Tara, I've been thinking about you a lot. Because . . . because I'd like to tell you how I feel."

"About Susie?"

"About you, Tara. And by the way, this is Susie's idea. She told me I've been taking you for granted for years. She gave me quite a lecture, actually. She's the one who made me realize how much I really care about you."

I held completely still and stared at Ethan in amazement, my heart flooding. Oh, Susie, I thought. Have you known all along?

"When did you talk to Susie?" I asked cautiously.

"I talk to her all the time. I talked to her yesterday. I needed her to coach me through this."

This made me laugh. It was an old thing with us. We'd coached each other for years. Susie coached Ethan and me through high school Spanish. Ethan coached me through physics. I coached Susie through math. Now we were coaching each other through life.

Ethan was still talking. I watched his face, this face that I loved so much. "I talked to Susie yesterday. Did she tell you her latest scheme? She wants to go to South America, on some church medical mission thing."

90

I didn't know this. How could Susie be making such a big decision and I didn't even know about it? But, it fits. It sounded just like Susie. I guess I was not surprised at all. I recalled that when she didn't buy that horse, her parents wanted her to save the money for college. But instead she gave it to their church mission. Some missionaries had visited their church and the slides of the children had made her cry. Yes, it fit. But why didn't she tell me? Or maybe she did and I just didn't put two and two together.

"Look, Tara, Susie and I are still friends. She is a great woman. But she has things she wants to do, and I am staying right here and I want to spend a lot of time catching up with you." Ethan looked into my eyes and waited for an answer.

I couldn't ignore the waves of happiness that surged through me. But then my practical self took over. "Ethan, you just got home. Wait and see how you feel after you've been here awhile.

"Okay," said Ethan seriously. "That makes sense. But don't move away, okay? Promise me that you won't move away. At least not anytime soon." Now he was holding both of my hands in his, as if he thought I might move away that very instant.

I smiled. "Move away? Are you kidding? I just put in a garden."

I was thinking about tomato sauce and Ethan, and my bedroom filled with streams of pale, coral light.

THE END

MILITARY HONOR

I Was Forced To Leave My Newborn Twins

I'd always been a patriotic person. My dad had been in the military, and Uncle Chad had made it his career. My cousins had lived all over the United States and in Germany. When terrorists destroyed the World Trade Center and attacked the Pentagon on September 11th, everything changed.

I'd been one of those people mesmerized by the destruction and despair. I couldn't stop watching the television news. I had been upset and unhappy, but I wanted to do something. I'd needed to help.

I decided to join the Army Reserves. I had been a single woman and a nurse. I knew that I could really assist and help my country. A month later, I went to a recruiting officer and talked to a Sergeant about joining the Reserves.

They were thrilled to have me because I had already been trained as a nurse. They rushed me through the paperwork and said that they would be contacting me shortly. I had been pleased that I was doing my part to help our country.

Basic training hadn't been fun, but I learned a lot about myself. I would be able to endure difficulties if I had to face them. Of course, I hadn't expect to do anything other than work one weekend a month on a base.

I loved the idea of helping my country, so I hadn't expected to become friends with some of the other reservists.

"I have the perfect guy for you, my twin brother, Michael," Michelle, my new reservist's friend said.

"I don't want to meet anyone—especially on a blind date," I said.

"It wouldn't be a blind date. He's coming to pick me up today. Once he meets you, I'm sure he'll ask you out," she said confidently.

Before I could respond, I noticed a tall, dark-haired man looking in my direction. Maybe he's a new reservists, I thought. He continued to walk in my direction, and he was smiling broadly.

"Hi," he said. "Are you ready to go?"

"In a sec," Michelle said. "I want you to meet my friend—"

"And you must be Angelica," he said. "She talks about you all the time." Then he offered me his hand.

"Yes," I managed to utter. His handshake was firm but warm. Somehow, I knew my life was going to change.

"We're going out for a few beers," he said. "Would you like to join us?"

"Sure," I replied. "I was getting ready to leave anyway. Just let me get my gear. I'll follow you in my car."

Michelle gave me one of those "I-told-you-so looks." I thought her brother was charming, but I hadn't been looking for romance. I was thirty-two years old, and been burned by romance too many times. I'd just wanted my life to be peaceful and helpful. That was one of the reasons I loved being a nurse.

Michael drove to a pub about forty minutes away from the base. Before I knew it, I had been laughing and relaxing in a way I hadn't in years.

"Do you think Shelly is trying to set us up?" he asked.

"Yep," I replied.

"This time I agree with her choice," he said softly as he placed his hand over mine. I could feel the heat emanating from him. "I'd really like to get to know you. May I see you this weekend?"

"Yes," I said without thinking. Would he think I was desperate? That wasn't the impression I wanted to leave with him. "Uh, why don't you call me?" I backtracked.

"Just slide me the digits, and I'll call you tonight."

I gave him my phone number, but I hadn't expected him to call. I'd never understood why men asked for your telephone number when they didn't plan on calling you. I liked Michael but he seemed a little too sure of himself, a little too charming. I'd met his type before.

Later that evening, after a shower, the phone rang. It had been unusual for me to get a late call, unless it was the hospital. I had been a single woman without children or other responsibilities so I had been called often to fill in when someone was out sick. Although I loved my job, I had been tired. I hadn't wanted to work.

"Hello," I answered reluctantly.

"Is this Angelica Melendes?" an unfamiliar voice asked.

"Yes," I said hesitantly. I hope this isn't one of those telemarketers. I'm really not up to a call tonight.

"This is Michael, Shelly's brother."

"Oh, hi," I said.

"I hope I haven't called you at a bad time," he said. "I just wanted to hear your voice again."

"Please, you don't have to pour on the charm," I said.

"I really had a great time with you tonight. I didn't want it to end, but I knew you were tired. I really wanted to hear your voice."

Michael and I must have talked for three hours. By the time our conversation ended, it was already past midnight. That was the first of many late-night conversations. Before I knew it, I had been swept off my feet.

93

Michael and I were a couple, and Michelle was thrilled. "Finally, I'll get a sister-in-law," she said.

"I think it's a little early for that," I replied.

"I don't know. He asked me what kind of diamond rings women like. That sounds pretty serious to me."

And Michael and I were serious. I hadn't wanted to talk about it. I had been a little superstitious, and I hadn't wanted to jinx it. We had talked about our future and the children we would have. Since neither of us was young, we wanted to start a family right away.

"I can't wait to see you pregnant with my child," he said.

"Well, I can wait. I'm probably going to be as huge as a house. You'll have to tie my laces because I won't be able to reach my shoes," I quipped.

"You know I'd do anything for you. I'll even make those midnight runs to the store for ice cream when you start to have cravings."

Until I'd met Michael, I hadn't known that I could be so comfortable with another person. Michael was a salesperson for a paper manufacturer. He was friendly and easygoing, the exact opposite of me. I had been still shy and a little intense. But we agreed on the big things. We both wanted to raise a family, have a house in the suburbs, and take family vacations.

And Michael made me feel things in bed that I'd never experienced. His boudoir intensity made me blush in and out of bed. We'd spent passion-filled evenings where we whispered our private dreams for the future.

One day Michael began joking about our future lives. His facial expression became serious as he continued to speak. "Do you think you've known me long enough to get married?"

"Are you asking me to marry you?" I joked.

"Only if you're saying, yes," he said. Then he clasped my hand and pulled moved toward him. "Angelica, I never thought I'd meet a woman like you. You're everything I've ever wanted. I know that we haven't known each other that long, but I can't imagine living without you. Please, marry me," he said.

"Oh, yes," I said between tears.

We began planning our wedding immediately. I had been an only child and my parents were dead. I'd thought that we'd have a small ceremony and have dinner with a few close friends afterward.

"Are you joking?" Michael asked. "I want the whole world to know how much I love you. I want you to plan the wedding you've always wanted!"

"But all I want is you," I said.

"That's why I love you so much," he said. "I'll help you do plan it. I see a church with lots of flowers and a violinist playing as the wedding party enters. Don't cheat yourself, Angie. You deserve all that and more."

I hadn't thought about having a big wedding, but I'd realized that was what Michael wanted. We'd agreed to compromise. We'd have a church wedding with flowers and violinist, but we'd have a small wedding party—only a maid of honor and a best man. And we'd have fewer than one hundred people at the reception. I'd told him that I hadn't wanted to wait a year, and neither had he. He told me that we'd get married in six months.

I'd spent the next three months in a fog. I continued with my reservist unit and my job. But I hadn't accepted overtime, and I'd let my supervisor know that I wouldn't be available to fill-in any longer. I'd wanted to spend as much time as I could with Michael.

I had been preparing a special dinner for Michael and me. I had come from the doctor and discovered that I had been pregnant. I knew Michael would be as happy as I had been. Then the phone rang.

It's probably Michael calling to tell me he's going to be late, again, I thought.

"Hi," I answered.

"Oh, Angelica. You have to come now," Michelle said between sobs. "It's Michael."

"Where are you? What happened?"

"He had a heart attack. I'm at St. Jude's. Please hurry."

I'd turned off the oven and dashed out the house. When I'd arrived at the hospital, I ran to Michelle. Between cries, she told me that Michael had a massive heart attack. Before the night ended, Michael was gone.

I don't remember the funeral or burial. I think the only thing that kept me going was the pregnancy. I had become concerned because I'd gained a lot of weight early on. Then the doctor told me that I was having twins. Twins, and I hadn't been able to share the good news with Michael. I'd missed him so much.

Michelle was terrific. She went with me for doctor visits and practically moved in. "I have to look out for my nephew and niece," she said.

When the babies were born, I cried. I was happy that there weren't complications and the children were well. I'd named them Michael Anthony Caldwell, Jr. and Shelly Antonia Caldwell. I'd loved my babies, but I'd missed Michael desperately. I'd wanted him to share that moment with me. Michelle had been with me during the entire birthing, but it hadn't been the same.

I dried my tears and told Michelle that I needed to rest. She'd kissed my cheek and thanked me for making her an aunt.

I had taken a short maternity leave from my job and the reserves.

Michelle had been great. She'd even found me a baby-sitter for the children.

"I don't want you to worry about the babies. She comes highly recommended and she's available."

Mrs. Brunson was a godsend. Not only was she great with the children, but she was terrific with me. She always had a word of encouragement. She treated me as though I was a member of her family—and I really needed that support.

She had started taking care of the children a few weeks before I was to return to work.

"I need to get to know the babies and the babies need to get to know me. And you need to start resting more. I know what a handful twins can be. I have a pair of my own. I remember those first crazy months, so I really understand what you're going through."

I was so busy with the twins and grieving, I hadn't paid much attention to the changes in the unit. Suddenly, we were doing more combat training.

Michelle showed some signs of concern. "What plans have you made for the twins? You know, the military always asks for a contingency plan."

"Of course, if something were to happen to me I'd want you to be their guardian."

"No, I mean if the unit gets called."

"I'm not going to get called. I have babies at home."

A few months later our unit was called to serve. I hadn't expected it, and I wasn't prepared for it. I'd been trained to handle combat, but I hadn't thought about the emotional turmoil I would be faced if I had to leave my children.

I came home sobbing. When Mrs. Brunson asked what was wrong, I explained the problem. She made me a cup of tea and told me everything would be all right.

"I'm going to take care of the babies like I do know. So, don't worry. We'll just stay here. I wouldn't desert them or you. You're a courageous woman, and I want you to know that I'm here for you."

I was so grateful; I just sat there and cried again. Now, I'm on my way overseas. I already miss my babies. When they grow up, I want them to know that I loved my country enough to help.

Of course, I'm scared. I don't know what's going to happen. I pray that the war ends soon, so I can return home. But if I don't come home, I know my babies will be loved and care for.

THE END

A SOLDIER'S STORY
His Love Helped Me
Conquer War And Disability

Reports of suicide bombs and insurgent rebels fill newspaper articles and the television news shows, nightly. As a soldier headed for the Middle East, I received extensive training about them before my unit was deployed. We were fighting a different kind of war—a different kind of enemy who didn't mind dying for his cause. And he didn't care if he took you and anyone else in the vicinity right along with him. He'd even use an innocent child to do his dirty work.

Iraqi insurgents fought their battles with improvised explosive devices, better known as IEDs. They were the weapons of choice, and were responsible for the majority of American deaths from hostile forces. At the beginning of the war, they were constructed with old artillery shells, nine-volt batteries, and pink Soviet detonation cords and filled with nails, screws, and needles designed to inflict even more damage. They were often daisy-chained together with collapsible circuits that made them particularly difficult to disarm.

Now, the bombs were becoming more sophisticated as their makers learned new skills. The latest wireless technology that allowed the average American to open his garage door from three houses down or make a cross-country call on a cell phone, now allowed an insurgent to detonate a bomb using a remote.

March tenth dawned like any other day. My buddies and I trooped to the mess hall for our usual breakfast of eggs, bacon, and toast peppered with a fine layer of desert sand—something you couldn't escape, no matter how hard you tried.

My unit was responsible for performing routine surveillance in Baghdad, which had six million people crammed into eighty-one square miles of filth and the foul-smelling remnants of two decades of war.

Every day was pretty much the same. Eat, sleep, go on patrol, service our weapons, and maintain the equipment. After each long day, we'd return to our quarters and try to scrub off the grime and cool off, but with little success at either.

Every day, we made the rounds of the same streets and saw the same faces. Yet despite the boredom, there was a certain comfort in that sameness. We became acquainted with some of the locals and made a special effort to interact with the kids. We figured if we could win over the youngest generation, maybe we'd stand a chance in another decade or two.

But all the routine and goodwill in the world couldn't counteract the unconscionable act of someone with an uncommon view on life and an unusual set of standards.

As we maneuvered down a familiar street, I spied a group of small boys playing with a ball we'd given them a few days earlier. When they heard the rumble of our vehicles, they paused and cleared the way for us. When we had candy, we'd stop and pass out lollipops and bubblegum. If time allowed, we'd engage them in a pickup game of soccer.

There was no time for games and candy that day because we'd received word of an abandoned car in a side alley and needed to check it out before we called in an explosive ordnance disposal tech team. Locating it proved easy—perhaps a little too easy in retrospect—but the alley was too narrow for our vehicle, so Teddy Barfield and I scrambled out of the Humvee and made our way to the car. One of the youngsters called to us and began walking into the alley, full of boyish eagerness and curiosity.

"Get back," I cautioned, my weapon in one hand, and waving him back with the other. I approached the non-descript sedan, observed the infant seat in the rear, and leaned toward the car to peer into the window.

Suddenly, there was a loud boom and a brilliant flash. That's the last thing I remembered until I woke up in a field station—my body battered, bruised, and scorched. My eyes were bandaged, and my future looked very bleak.

The field station and Forward Surgical Team stabilized me. Two days later, they hustled me onto a plane to Landstuhl Army Regional Medical Center,near Ramstein Air Base in Germany—had better facilities to treat my injuries. At LARMC, I was seen by so many specialists, that I lost count. Most of them had titles I couldn't pronounce if I tried.

Their immediate concerns were my eye injuries and the shrapnel that had penetrated my skull. An infectious disease specialist cautioned that I might develop infections later from the bomb as bits of debris worked their way to the surface of my skin. A plastic surgeon was also brought in to evaluate future reconstructive surgery on my face. Finally, the shrink dropped by for a visit and told me I should talk about my feelings and get everything off my chest.

Yeah, right.

The next weeks were a blur of doctors, surgeries, therapy, and that damned shrink. And every time I closed my eyes, I re-lived the explosion. When the pain would surface, I'd ask for more pills and hope they'd stop the dreams, too. By the time I ended up stateside at Walter Reed a month later, I was as ornery as a stray dog with a sore paw.

You're still a young woman, Chelsea. There are a lot of things you can do, baby girl. Those were the words from my father and I suppose they were his way of encouraging me.

Be thankful you're still alive. Easy for the chaplain to say when he stopped by everyday to pray for my sorry soul. I had to wonder just how alive I could be if I couldn't see the world around me.

Corporal Nolan, there's a chance, though it's a very small percentage, that you'll have some residual vision. I don't want to promise anything though. That less-than-encouraging verdict was delivered by the latest eye specialist who had examined my wounds and recommended I be medically retired.

I'd often heard there were no atheists in foxholes, and I was about to believe there were none with their names emblazoned on medical retirement forms either. I was hanging onto obscure hope, and between pity parties, I tried to remember the words to any prayer I'd ever heard and bargained with a God that I'd negligently allowed to slide into the background of my life. If God worked a miracle and my sight was fully returned, I could remain a soldier. If it didn't, I was out in the big, cold, dark world, and it was my own damned fault!

I'd been in the last month of my tour of duty. That's when fatigue, distraction, and homesickness were most likely to set in. All I could focus on was shipping out and seeing something besides sand and destruction. I was eager to see my family again, and anxious to resume the life I'd left when I dropped out of college four years, earlier.

The Army awarded me a Purple Heart for my injuries, and a Gold Star because I saved that kid and dragged my partner away from the burning vehicle. Apparently, I even tried to save the guy who had detonated the bomb—probably so I could make sure the SOB was punished for his actions.

My mom pinned the medals on my hospital issued pajamas and blubbered on about how proud she was of me. My dad didn't say much, but I could hear the sorrow in his voice. I'd never seen my father cry, but I could have sworn I heard him sniff a couple times. When my folks left, I yanked the medals off, extended my arm as far as it would go, and dropped them with a clank onto the floor beside my bed.

"Corporal, these must have slipped off your bed while you were sleeping," the nurse making rounds said, scooping them from the floor.

"What should I do with them?" she inquired.

"I don't give a damn what you do with them, lady. Just get them the hell out of here!" I snapped.

The Army should have awarded me the Medal of Stupidity and

a Commendation of Carelessness instead, because I sure deserved it. I should have known that car was a trap. It fit every profile I'd been taught.

I'd been distracted. I had zigged when I should have zagged.

Now, I was being medically retired from the service; and when I wasn't re-living the bombing, I was lying in bed with antibiotics dripping through an IV—wondering what a third-generation soldier did when she wasn't a soldier, anymore.

The door to my room whooshed open, and I heard the whisper of rubber soles against the freshly mopped vinyl floor. Just an hour earlier—or had it been longer or shorter? How did you tell when you couldn't see the clock? Someone had scurried in, and a disembodied voice with a thick, southern accent apologized for disturbing me while she cleaned the room. The nauseating iodine smell of the cleansers still hung heavily in the air and overpowered everything else until the door opened again. I smelled meat, hot bread, and something with chocolate.

"Lunchtime!"

I grunted and lay perfectly still. The food they'd been bringing me—and it was an exaggeration to call it food—was as bland as wallpaper paste. I wanted to call Teddy and ask him to swing by a greasy spoon and bring me a double jumbo cheeseburger with everything on it. I could almost taste the tang of the mustard and the bite of raw onion. But Teddy didn't make it after I dragged him away from the burning car.

And I hadn't even been able to attend his funeral!

Despite growing up on opposite sides of the country, we'd led amazingly parallel lives. Our fathers and grandfathers had served in the Army, we'd both gone to college when we finished high school, and we'd both decided to drop out and enlist after the terrorist attacks on September eleventh.

Maybe Teddy was the lucky one. Every time I touched the gauzy bandages that covered my eyes, I wondered what was in store for me. In less than a month, I was already having difficulty remembering what some things looked like. If fate dealt me the wrong percentage, and I didn't have the residual vision the specialist talked about, would I forget completely?

"Sugar, how are you gonna get out of here if you don't eat?"

"Well, well, well. If it's not Nurse Perky," I mocked. "Maybe I don't wanna get out of here. Maybe I'll just rot in this awful place."

I grunted again as she pressed the buttons on the control pad clipped to my pillow, and I heard the hospital bed whir into action and raise me to a sitting position.

"I'm not a nurse, Corporal," she corrected. "I'm just a dietary aide, and my name is Taylor."

"Well, I'm going to call you Nurse Perky, anyway. I like how it sounds," I decreed, not caring about protocol or manners. I was mad at the world and didn't care whose feelings I stomped on. Lashing out at others kept me from feeling my own pain—physical and emotional. "You're not going to argue with a wounded soldier, are you?"

I wasn't above playing the guilt card with anyone.

"I suppose it won't hurt," she said, and I heard her roll the tray to my bed. "You want me to feed you or you want to try it yourself, today?" She was so close that I could smell the minty gum she chewed.

A week of her solicitous behavior, combined with the haze of pain and the uncertainty of my life, exploded like that IED. I inched my fingers across the crisp cotton sheet until I felt the hard edge of the rolling hospital tray. I shoved it hard, and it skittered away from the bed—the contents clattering on the floor.

I heard the woman gasp, and I waited for her comments—ready to fire back with my own. But another voice spoke, instead.

"Guess I got here just in time for the show."

Jared.

The love of my life.

The man with whom I thought I would spend eternity.

The man I needed to drive away because he deserved better than a blind woman with no future!

"I'm Jared Miller," he said to the aide. "I'm Chelsea's fiancé. And I'd like to apologize for her obnoxious behavior."

"I'm Taylor Owens, Mr. Miller. And well . . . she's just acting out her anger. I see it every day in here."

"She may be angry, Ms. Owens, but that's no reason to make your job any harder or to act like a spoiled child."

Jared always did have a way of getting right to the heart of things.

"Get outta here. Both of you!"

I barked orders like a drill sergeant.

I heard rubber soles squeal against the floor as the aide made a hasty exit. Then, I heard the staccato click of boot heels crossing the room.

"I asked you to leave!" I repeated.

I was sightless and tethered to the bed by an IV, or I would have personally escorted Jared to the door.

"If you weren't hooked to that IV, I'd make you get your sorry butt out of the bed and clean up this mess."

"I asked you to leave," I repeated, my teeth clenched tightly, and my hand grasping a fistful of the bed sheet.

"No, you ordered me to leave. I don't take orders from spoiled brats!"

Jared's voice was cool and edgy.

Lord only knows why I was picking a fight with him; but lately, I

101

seemed hell bent on destroying everything that was sacred. I'd driven my mother away in tears, and thus, incurred the wrath of my father. I'd sniped at every nurse, orderly, and aide who'd had the misfortune to come near me. The last time the psychiatrist paid me a visit, I'd told him where to take his mumbo-jumbo and shove it!

But Jared? He didn't deserve my bad mood. He didn't deserve to be treated like anything but the gentleman he was. But he also didn't deserve to be saddled with me.

We'd met in a math class during the spring semester of our sophomore year at Vanderbilt University. I was there on a full academic scholarship and majoring in political science, with plans to attend law school after graduation. Jared was an English major and smart as a whip, but numbers eluded him. When he asked me for help, how could I turn down the sexiest, most handsome man I'd ever met?

His wavy, black hair and whiskey color made him stand out among a sea of blond, blue-eyed jocks. After a few tutoring sessions, I found myself falling for him, but held out no hope that a sophisticated city boy from Richmond would even consider dating a Tennessee farm girl like me.

Jared surprised me, though.

"You might come from a small town, Chelsea Nolan, but your goals are world-class."

Unlike so many boys who never gave me a second look because I didn't sport a sorority pin and designer labels, Jared looked beyond the external and into my heart—a heart that was his almost from the beginning.

We had no idea that our time together would be so short. After the September 11th attacks, I knew I couldn't sit in a university classroom studying about government and freedom when our own was under attack. My folks persuaded me to at least complete my third year of college, but that's all I agreed to.

Jared pleaded with me not to leave.

"You can be a freedom fighter right here at home," he begged. "And what about law school?"

"Baby, I can finish that when I get out of the Army," I assured him. "Besides, what good is law if we have no freedom?"

The evening before I left for basic training, we drove to Centennial Park and walked hand-in-hand around the Parthenon. We picnicked on deli sandwiches and fruit, then lay side by side on a blanket under a darkening sky, and wished on the first star.

"Penny for your thoughts," I teased.

When he looked at me, his eyes were filled with anguish.

"I've quit wishing that you'll change your mind. So I can only wish that you'll stay safe and come back to me."

He pulled me into his arms, and I felt his heart pounding next to mine.

"Of course, I'll come back to you," I promised.

"Will you also promise to marry me when you return?"

My eyelashes were damp with unshed tears, and all I could do was nod.

To seal that promise, he pulled his grandmother's engagement ring from his pocket. His gaze shifted from my face to the ring and back to my face. I pressed my fingers to my lips, and the previously unshed tears tracked down my cheeks.

"I hope that's a yes."

His voice was filled with uncertainty.

I nodded and smiled.

"That's absolutely a yes."

"I love you, Jared," I professed as he slipped the sparkling ring on my finger. "I'll always love you, no matter what."

I still loved him, but I couldn't hold him to any promises, now. He'd graduated from Vandy with honors. Then, he received his Master's degree, and an offer to stay in the Nashville area and teach at a community college.

"I think maybe I have a right to be a little spoiled. Don't you understand what's happened to me?"

"Look at yourself, Chelsea. You—"

"Well, that's where we have a little problem, darlin'," I snapped. "I can't look at anything, right now."

"I'm speaking metaphorically, darling—"

"You need to use smaller words, sweetheart. I didn't graduate from college like you did."

"And whose fault is that?" he asked.

I clawed at the edge of my pillow and found the plastic call box clipped to the pillowcase. I'd finished with the verbal sparring, and I mashed the button repeatedly until a staticky voice responded.

"Yes, Corporal Nolan?"

"I thought I told you to put a No Visitors sign on my door."

"We did, Corporal."

"It must not be big enough because I have a visitor."

I'd hoped to drive him from the room in anger, but Jared hadn't budged.

"I'm sorry, Corporal. I'll—"

"I'm sick of your damned excuses!" I yelled in a voice loud enough to be heard clear to the Pentagon. I seized the call box, yanked it free from the pillowcase, and hurled it toward the foot of my bed. Only the cord connecting it to the wall prevented it from becoming the latest victim of my rage.

The clicking heels moved closer, and the odor of sickness was replaced by the scent of Jared. He placed his hand on my arm, and I pulled away as if it were a blistering ember. Then, the fragrance of spice and citrus grew stronger, and his lips gently grazed my cheek.

"Go away, Jared!" I ordered, treating him like a raw recruit. "I don't want you here. I don't need you here."

I turned my head and faced away from him.

"What if I don't want to go away?" he countered, his fingers gently touching the bandage on my eyes, and then, blazing a trail to my lips. "What if I think you do need me here? What are you going to do if I park my butt in the chair in the corner and refuse to leave until you come to your senses and see that this isn't the end of your life?"

"Park away, sweetheart," I said sarcastically, digging into my memory for images of his broad shoulders and trim waist. "Just please spare me the 'it could be worse,' speech. Been there, done that, waiting for the T-shirt to arrive."

"When your dad called me and told me about the bomb, I went completely numb. Even though he told me you were still alive, I don't think I really believed him until I walked into this room. I've tried to call you. I've sent you cards and gifts and flowers—which I might add—have gone unacknowledged."

He paused to draw in a deep breath, and my attempt to interrupt was promptly cut short.

"I'm going to have my say, Chelsea, and you can just keep your mouth shut till I'm finished."

He was on a roll, and when I dug way back into the recesses of my memory, I recalled how his brown eyes would darken when he was passionate about an issue.

"You've been a selfish bitch, throwing yourself a gigantic pity party, and forgetting how this has affected the people who love you."

I could hear his heels tap against the vinyl floor as he spoke and paced back and forth, and back again. Something jangled as he walked. Car keys, perhaps? Or loose change in his pocket?.

"Your mother worries about how you're going to manage once the hospital releases you, and your father is probably going to end up with an ulcer the size of Texas because he keeps everything bottled up inside. But he worries about you, Chelsea." His voice grew softer as he continued. "I worry about you, too. If you'd make even a little effort, we'd all rest a little easier."

I said nothing, waiting for him to continue with the diatribe.

"I know how you must feel—"

"Now, that's where you're wrong, Jared." I gritted my teeth and twisted the rough edge of the hospital blanket. "There's no way in hell you know how I feel. I gave up everything I knew, and now, I've had it all taken away. If I'm lucky, I might be able to see a few shadows. Even at that, I'll spend the rest of my life with a white cane, listening to people whisper behind my back about how pathetic I am. I can't go back, and I can't go forward. So you tell me, Mr. Know-It-All, what the hell am I going to do besides sell pencils on a street corner?"

I felt something land on my lap. I fumbled around and my fingers made contact with a piece of paper covered with rough patches.

"What the hell is this?"

"If you'd gone to your therapy sessions, you'd know it's Braille. And would you please stop cursing?"

"I'll say what I damn well—"

"Please, Chelsea."

His voice was thick with emotion.

"I talked with someone last week who told me that you can still go to law school if you want," he continued. "You can be anything you set your mind to—if you're just willing to work hard. And I know you can work hard, Chelsea."

His voice possessed a tone of defiance, as well as a subtle challenge.

A part of me buried deep knew he was right. But it was easier to give up. Simpler to throw temper tantrums. The edge of the narrow mattress dipped, and I smelled the spicy aftershave again, as he kissed me softly.

"You can throw all the temper tantrums you want, Chelsea Nolan, but nothing will make me stop loving you." His voice cracked, and I felt a tear slide from his cheek to mine. "I thank God every day for letting you survive that bombing and come home to me."

I swallowed against a lump in my throat and struggled to speak.

"Jared," I said, my voice cracking with despair and anger. "You deserve better than a stubborn jackass like me."

He stretched out on the bed and settled his warm, muscular body next to mine.

"Shh. You may be right, but you're my stubborn jackass, and you're not getting rid of me anytime, soon."

He kissed me, again—this time nibbling at my lips and then deepening the kiss with an emotion that spoke volumes. I knew then I wanted to be the best blind person I could, to meet his silent challenge and prove that I could still be the woman he'd fallen in love with years earlier.

At three a.m., the nurse who came in for her middle-of-the-night check, awakened me. Jared still lay beside me—his head on my shoulder, and his breath warm against my neck.

Busted.

I listened as the nurse checked my IV and vital signs and

105

scribbled the necessary notations on my chart. I figured the reprimand was coming next, so I decided to beat her to the punch.

"I'll wake him up and get him out of here," I whispered. "We didn't mean to break any rules. It's just that he traveled so far and we lost track of time and—"

She took my hand in hers and gave it a quick squeeze.

"Go back to sleep," she said, softly. "You need your rest."

Her shoes squeaked across the floor and just before the door closed with a gentle snick, she called back to me.

"Rules were meant to be broken, young lady. Especially when you've been blinded by love."

THE END